STRIKE TWO

Amy Goldman Koss
STRIKE TWO

Dial Books
New York

Many thanks to Lauri Hornik, Clara Rodriguez,
Jacki Doi, and Mitch Koss

Published by Dial Books
A division of Penguin Putnam Inc.
345 Hudson Street
New York, New York 10014
Copyright © 2001 by Amy Goldman Koss
All rights reserved
Designed by Lily Malcom
Text set in Bembo
Printed in the U.S.A. on acid-free paper
1 3 5 7 9 10 8 6 4 2

Library of Congress Cataloging-in-Publication Data
Koss, Amy Goldman, date.
Strike two / by Amy Goldman Koss.
p. cm.
Summary: Gwen's hope of spending the summer playing softball
and hanging out with her cousin Jess is ruined when her father and
her uncle land on opposite sides of the local newspaper strike.
ISBN 0-8037-2607-4
[1. Strikes and lockouts—Fiction.   2. Softball—Fiction.
3. Cousins—Fiction.]   I. Title.
PZ7.K8527 Sv 2001
[Fic]—dc21 00-038365

*To Max and
Harriet Goldman
with love*

CONTENTS

Chapter One
THE PICKET LINE

IT WAS SO hot and sticky that none of us could concentrate. First Vicky let loose an enormous sigh and dropped to her knees in the outfield. Then Marsha tipped over at second base. When my cousin Jess peeled off her shin guards and plopped down on the pitcher's mound, that was it—the rest of us also fell to the ground.

Coach Marty called out, "Yeah, but what if this was a game?"

"We'd play," Linea yelled back.

"We'd win," I added.

"You'll see," Joy agreed.

So Coach Marty threw his glove in the air and sank down

like the rest of us. The few parents in the stands laughed. Then everyone crawled off the field, got into cars, and added themselves to the roaring traffic.

But Aunt Ann was late, so Jess and I had to scrunch into the pitiful inch of shade from the bleachers and watch the *Press Gazette*'s boys' team warm up. They thought they were so great—especially that guy Abe. I tried not to watch him catch the ball behind his back, under his knee, and all that. He was a big show-off.

Jess picked up her invisible telephone, thumb to her ear, pinky to her mouth. "Hello?" she said.

I automatically held mine. We'd been doing this since birth. "Hello. Who's this?"

"It's me. Where's my mom?" asked Jess.

I shrugged. "I don't know. But I'm starving!"

"And *thhhhhirsty,*" Jess said in a Daffy Duck voice.

Finally, Aunt Ann pulled up and we lunged for the backseat. *Ahhh,* air-conditioning!

"Mom," Jess said, "it's a Pizza Pete's Emergency!"

Her baby brother Riley's eyes lit up. "Pia Pee!" he cheered, rocking in his car seat. "Pia Pee!"

Jess and I joined the chant. "PIA PEE! PIA PEE!"

But Aunt Ann shook her head, aimed the car toward my house, and said, "Sorry, guys. Maybe next time."

And when we both tumbled out of the car and headed up my walk, Aunt Ann called Jess back.

"We're not going in? Even for a second?" Jess asked.

"Not today," Aunt Ann said with a fake-looking smile. So Jess got back into the car and they were gone.

• • •

I went straight to the fridge and pulled out grapes, cheese, leftover pasta salad, and a carton of milk. Carefully balancing my loot, I closed the door with my hip—and was startled by the sight of *Dad,* grinning at me. I almost dropped everything. "What are *you* doing here?" I asked, joining him at the table.

"Having a wee snack," he said, pointing to his gigantic half-eaten sandwich and mound of cole slaw. He poked his fork out to nab some of my pasta salad and asked how my practice went—as if his being home in the middle of the day was perfectly normal.

I told him Coach Marty drilled us in fielding, then I asked again, "But why are you home?"

Mom appeared in the kitchen door. "The newspaper went on strike today," she told me. "Just till both sides agree on a new contract."

I must've looked confused, because she said, "Every four years they have to negotiate a new contract and hammer out things like hours, salary, medical benefits, sick days, vacations, stuff like that."

I nodded with my mouth full of grapes, and Dad added, "Our old contract expired a month ago. The unions said we'd stop work if there wasn't a new one by today—and there wasn't, so here I am."

"Great!" I said. "You can come to our game next Tuesday!"

Dad was a copy editor, and he worked all hours, fixing articles that were turned in late. He'd only seen me play softball *twice* all last summer.

"The strike won't last that long," he said. "We scared the pants off them today! You should've seen their faces when we walked out." Dad twirled an invisible villain mustache and cackled. "By tomorrow they'll be on their knees, begging us to come back."

"I certainly hope so," Mom said.

Dad pointed his fork at me. "Meanwhile, kid, you and I walk the picket line tonight!"

"Me? Cool!" I pictured myself marching with a big sign. "Is Jess coming?"

My parents looked at each other. Then Dad said, "Nope."

"But Uncle Dave works at the paper," I said.

"He's management, Gwen," Mom explained. "They don't strike." I frowned, and she added, "Management are the bosses and department heads. Everyone else, like Dad, are the workers. Not that Uncle Dave isn't a *worker*, but . . ."

Dad laughed. "He's the *bad guys*. He's on the *other* team."

Uncle Dave was Dad's twin brother. When they played each other at *anything*—cards, volleyball, whatever—they did a lot of name-calling and accused each other of cheating. They were both bragging winners and sore losers. Jess and I refused to play with them. I could definitely imagine them on opposite sides of this strike, razzing each other.

The picket line was even better than I thought it would be. It was like a giant party. And no one mentioned how late it was, or how I should be home in bed. I only wished Jess had been there. She would've loved it.

I recognized people from Dad's office and a few parents of girls on my team. Even Coach Marty was there. He tossed me an imaginary ball and I pretended to swing. Then he stood around joking with my dad and some police officers.

Being there on the plaza at night reminded me of the newspaper's Fourth of July party, a yearly favorite for Jess and me. We'd always start by hanging around in the crowd on the plaza, eating snow cones and watching the jugglers and other street performers. But as soon as it got dark, we'd go inside the *Press Gazette* building and ride the elevator all the way up till our ears popped.

The doors would open on a huge room full of newspaper families drinking from fancy glasses and eating little sandwiches off silver trays. Jess and I would wiggle past them to the windows and look way down. From the top floor, the crowd looked like an amoeba oozing onto the plaza. The boats on the lake were as tiny as fireflies.

But there was nothing small about the fireworks. BOOM! I'd feel the first one in my belly as the sky burst into color. *"Ohhh! Ahhh!"* the whole room would say in unison.

Jess and I had named our favorite fireworks. The purple kind that fizzed into blue sparks were La-la-linas. We called the gold curlicue ones Loopy-la-las. (Ever since we were babies, we'd thought names that began with *L* were the most beautiful and romantic.)

Then the finale would arrive: boom boom boom boom— the rocket's red glare. Bombs bursting in air. And next: nothing. The silence would tingle in my ears. It gave me chills every single year, and there at the picket line I got chills again just *thinking* about it.

Then that boy Abe was suddenly standing next to me and I felt my heart go flip! He said, "Gwen, right?"

"Right," I said.

"Name's Abe," he said.

I nodded and didn't let on that I already knew not only his name, but where he went to school (which was Wilson, the middle school for extra-smart kids), what grade he was going to be in (eighth, which put him a year ahead of me), and that he played baseball.

Neither of us spoke for a while.

"They're union too," he finally said, nodding at the police officers. I didn't know what he meant.

"I'm half expecting fireworks," I said, then wanted to kick myself for sounding so dumb.

But Abe said, "Nah, I bet they settle the strike tonight. They're up there negotiating right now." He pointed to the lit windows in the *Press Gazette* building.

I tried to think of something strikish and intelligent to say back, but couldn't. Luckily, Vicky from my team came up to us just then with her hands full of donuts. She gave Abe a jelly-filled and me a glazed. She kept the chocolate.

Abe took a bite, then said, "Too gooey. Anybody wanna trade?"

I love jelly-filled. "Is it raspberry?" I asked.

He shrugged. "Dunno."

We swapped. I looked at his used donut and wondered

where to bite. Right next to *his* bite? Meanwhile he gobbled down my glazed donut and was licking his fingers when some guys yelled for him. He sauntered off in his show-offy way.

"You saving that for your scrapbook?" Vicky said with a giggle, pointing to the donut in my hand.

"Yick!" I squealed, and threw it in the trash.

Then Dad and Coach Marty called us over to the picket line. Vicky and I didn't get to carry signs or march, but we did get to chant: "What do we want? FAIR PAY! When do we want it? To-DAY!" We had a blast.

It was way too late to call Jess when we got home, so I had to wait until morning to tell her about everything.

"I wonder if *my* dad's side does anything fun," she said. "He never even came home from work last night."

"He worked all night long?" I thought of the lit windows. That must've been Uncle Dave up there. I wanted to tell Jess that if the strike lasted long enough, my dad would take us to Tuesday's game. But that seemed like bragging so instead I said, "Wanna go swimming or something?"

"Yeah," Jess said. "I'll ask my mom if she'll drive. Call you right back."

But when Aunt Ann arrived, Mom poured her a cup of coffee. Jess and I groaned; when the moms sit down and start yacking, all is lost. Aunt Ann plunked Riley down on the floor with a cup of Cheerios and waved Jess and me away as if we were flies.

Then I remembered I had an extra parent at home. We found Dad poking around in the yard and he agreed to drive us.

In the car Dad grinned at Jess. "Too bad *your* father can't come to the swim club! Poor, poor Dave stuck inside that stuffy old building on such a glorious day!" He snickered and twirled his imaginary mustache.

Jess and I rolled our eyes.

When we got to the pool, Dad didn't stay in the clubhouse with the other adults. He put on his trunks and came lumbering into the water as *Grim,* Evil Giant of the Deep! He growled and threw us around in the shallow end. Other kids came up to fight Grim too. It was a hoot!

That's my dad, I thought proudly.

The next day Dad offered to take Jess and me to a matinee.

"I'm missing all the fun," Mom said, refilling her coffee cup.

"Sorry, babe," Dad said.

Mom sighed and went back to her studio, which used to be our garage. She's a freelance graphic artist, meaning when she has assignments, she works like mad, and when she doesn't—she doesn't work at all. Too bad she has work while Dad is on strike, I thought, because otherwise she could come with us.

"Movie?" Dad said, breaking in on my thoughts.

"I don't know what's playing," I said. "I gotta look in the paper."

Dad blinked. "We don't have a paper, Gwen. We're on strike, remember?"

I didn't get it. "If there's no newspaper, what's Uncle Dave doing at work all the time?" I asked.

"Well, there's a *scab* paper," Dad said, wrinkling his nose in disgust. "But there will never be a scab paper in *this* house."

I pictured scabs on scraped knee and made a face.

Dad smiled. "Scabs are people who cross picket lines to do the strikers' work," he explained.

"Well, how do we know what movie is where?" I asked.

Dad laughed as if I were joking.

At the theater, he bought us whatever we wanted. I had a package of red licorice and a bag of Fritos. Jess had popcorn, soda, a candy bar, and some mints. Then she felt so sick that we had to leave before the end of the movie. But we'd already seen it, and Dad said he should get to the picket line anyway. He went every day. I wondered if that boy Abe would be there—but I didn't ask, of course.

The next day Dad took Jess and me to the beach and we got a parking space right near the sand. Dad was amazed; he was used to weekends when the place was mobbed and we had to park blocks away.

"Is the beach closed?" he asked. "Has the water been contaminated or something? Do you see any signs?"

Jess giggled.

We got out of the car. Dad kept looking around. "Where *is* everyone?" he asked. Then he said, "You sly little foxes! You had this whole secret world all to yourselves and we poor working stiffs had no idea what we were missing."

"Shhhh!" Jess said. "Don't tell anyone!"

When we were out for lunch afterward, Dad pointed to a man in a suit talking on a cell phone. "Did I look like that poor schmo?" he asked us.

Jess and I smiled at Dad's faded plaid shorts and wild Hawaiian shirt and said, "Yep."

He shuddered in horror and bought us all banana splits.

Chapter Two
STRIKES AND FOULS

THE STRIKE WASN'T over on Tuesday, so Dad took us to our first game. We'd been practicing forever—since before school even let out—and Jess and I were wildly excited. We looked great. Our uniforms would be rags by the end of the season, but for now they were bright and new—purple jerseys with PRESS GAZETTE stitched in yellow on the front and on our caps. The newspaper was our sponsor. We all had relatives who worked there.

Our home field was right next to the newspaper building. When Dad waved and honked at the picketers, Jess rolled down her window and stared. It occurred to me that this was probably the first time she'd seen the picket line, besides on TV.

"Uncle Bill?" she said as we parked. "Do you think the strike will—"

"No talk of the strike at the ball field!" Dad interrupted. "We're out of the strike zone!" He laughed at his pun.

I'd always envied Vicky because Coach Marty was her dad, but this time *my* dad was here too. He acted goofy, helping us warm up, and I could tell that everyone liked him.

Then Coach Marty called, "Bring it in!" and we all ran to him for our pregame pep talk. He used his serious coach voice when he said, "Look at one another. The faces in this circle belong to the most important people in your lives starting right now—and lasting till the final game of the season. Take a good look."

He waited so that we really would look at one another. A lot of us had played on the team together the year before, but some were new. We were from all over the city. Some girls went to my school (Lincoln), but the rest came from the three other middle schools.

When a few of the girls started to giggle and have stare-down contests, Coach Marty decided we'd looked at one another long enough. "You are a *team*!" he said. "That means you're all parts of a whole. Every part is equally essential. And all the parts have to work together. We're not looking for stars here, right? We're looking for teamwork! Okay. Break."

He stuck his fist in the center of the circle and we all piled our hands on top. Then we yelled, "PRESS GAZETTE! BEST TEAM YET! *GOOOOOOO* BLUE GIRLS! YAY!"

We ran to our positions (I was playing right field) and Coach Marty called, "Play ball!"

The Gas Company was up first, of course, because they were the visitors. And somehow, before we knew what hit us, *bam, bam, bam, bam,* the Gas Company had scored four runs off us! Just like that!

I'd have sworn that the first ball was a foul—but the ump called it fair. The second ball went right through Marsha's legs. The third was a bunt to first (which Liza and Joy both muffed). And the fourth batter brought them all home with a grand slam clear over the fence.

As the Gas Company went wild cheering, I looked at my teammates one by one. I couldn't tell about Corey behind her catcher's mask, but the rest looked entirely stupefied, with their mouths hanging open. I did too, probably.

Only Coach Marty looked calm. Still smiling, he called out, "Wake up, ladies! It's party time!" Finally something clicked and we pulled our fielding together. The next *bam, bam,* and *bam* were their three consecutive outs. Phew! We were up.

Then I spotted Gram in the stands. How could I have missed her? My grandmother was like a big solid boulder in the bleachers, and the cheering and twitching of the other spectators was just a brook babbling past.

I nudged Jess and we waved. Gram nodded back—one nod. Gram hated to waste nods.

Vicky was up first. She got a hit and Dad went berserk cheering, but that was nothing compared to the stomping and bellowing he did for Jess's double. When Joy struck out, Dad called the umpire a turkey, and when the Gas Company caught Linea's fly ball, I thought Dad was going to have a heart attack. I was up next.

We had two outs and two players on base, so the stakes were high. But I love pressure. I could already see myself on first base, down and ready. Then second! Third! Home! *Hooray!*

I swung and connected with a great pop! I loved that pop! I lived for that pop! I was halfway to first when the ump called, "*Strrrike* one. Foul ball!"

"No way!" Dad yelled. "Get your eyes checked, you bozo!" I knew other people were yelling too, but the only voice I heard was *Dad's*. I could feel my cheeks flaming.

I returned to home plate. I swung on the next one and missed! The ump called, "*Strrrike* two!"

Dad was hollering himself hoarse, and I was glad I couldn't make out his words. I peeked at Gram; she was expressionless.

"Choke up on it!" Linea growled from the dugout. I checked my hands. That bat was so choked up, its eyes were rolling. "Choke up on it!" she called again. I wanted to choke up on *her*.

"*Strike three!*" I'd blown it. I couldn't bear to face Dad or the girls I'd left on base. What a rotten way to start the season!

Vicky, whom I'd stranded on third, trotted up and said, "Bum luck, Gwen," in a sympathetic voice. That was nice of her, but I still felt lousy. And worse still when Linea said, "You gotta hold the bat way higher next time." I ignored her the best I could and headed for right field.

Jess pitched three up, three down in the second inning. We were all thrilled out of our gourds. Coach Marty called, "Hey, Jess, those lessons sure paid off!" and she smiled.

But then a man's voice yelled, "Helps to have a rich

daddy!" I saw Jess's smile freeze. I scanned the Gas Company fans, but no one was looking at us. I wondered if someone from *our* side could've said that.

Maybe I'd heard wrong or maybe the guy was just teasing. But from the expression on Jess's face, I knew *she* didn't take it as a joke.

I looked at Dad, but he was too busy doing his own yelling to have heard. Gram had one eyebrow raised, though, so I guess *she* had and didn't think it was funny.

I ran over to Jess and grabbed my invisible phone. "Hello?" Jess assumed the position. "Hello. Who's this?"

"The Baffle Bureau," I said.

"It was Marsha's dad," Jess whispered into her receiver. "I saw him." We looked at Marsha, but she was oblivious.

"I don't get it," I said.

Jess shrugged and we hung up.

I hoped Marsha's dad's comment wouldn't throw off Jess's timing. It didn't. If anything she pitched the rest of the game even better. And I made two hits (Phew!), so I stopped being bothered by Dad's rowdy cheering. We won eleven to four.

Afterward Gram offered to take all of us out for tacos. But Dad said he had to get to the picket line. That made Gram raise *both* eyebrows.

"Not to worry, Ma," Dad said. "A *little* picketing builds character."

Gram didn't look reassured. "A *little* picketing may build character," she said, "but more than that destroys it."

"The strike'll settle in no time," Dad answered, looking at his shoes—which was probably exactly what he did as a kid when Gram shook her finger at him. It always made me gig-gle when Gram shrunk Dad and Uncle Dave down like that. Jess and I secretly called it "Gram's Fountain of Youth."

"Fine, you build character, we'll eat tacos," Gram said. "Come on, girls." And off we went, leaving Dad alone scratching his head.

Some *Press Gazette* boys were taking the field, but I didn't see Abe—not that I would have done anything if he'd been there, except maybe said "Hi."

At Mr. Taco we got our usuals: a chicken quesadilla for me, the carne asada for Jess. Gram had a cup of coffee.

"Strikes were more dramatic and romantic in the old days," Gram said between sips. "About workers' rights and decent conditions. Now it's all money."

"I like money," Jess joked.

"I think the whole thing is just stupid," I said, expecting agreement.

But Gram said, "*Just* stupid? Stupidity alone has caused more anguish and destruction than any other single force on earth."

"Gram," I whined, "I'm sick and tired of all this strike talk. I thought we were celebrating Jess's brilliant pitching of the season's opener!"

"Not to mention Gwen's two incomparable hits!" Jess added.

Gram smiled and lifted her coffee cup to toast us, but I could tell that her thoughts were elsewhere.

And back in my room later, even the radio newswoman was talking about the strike. "The city is feeling the strain from the *Press Gazette* strike, now in day eight. Negotiations seem to have broken down and the bargaining committee is at an impasse. Union demands include a six percent raise over the next few years—with two percent the first year and the remaining four percent over the next three years."

Math! I thought. Fractions, no less. I *knew* there was something nasty about this strike. I clicked off the radio, letting the sound of crickets replace the newswoman's voice.

The next day Dad took Jess and me back to the beach. We buried him up to his neck, then Jess tickled his nose with a feather. Dad sneezed his giant Grim sneeze, burst out of the sand, and chased us into the lake.

I was getting a little tired of Grim, but Jess wasn't. She didn't seem to miss playing dolphins and mermaids with just me, like we did in the good old days when grown-ups sat on their blankets ignoring us unless we were drowning.

And I wouldn't have minded being ignored the next morning either. But Dad found me in the kitchen eating yogurt and asked if I wanted to go out for breakfast. He knows I'm not an out-to-breakfast person. In the morning I'm a stare-at-the-wall, shove-food-in-my-mouth kind of person.

"I'm already eating," I mumbled.

"Let's call Jess, see if she'd like to come," Dad said.

"Call her yourself," I answered.

Dad shrugged and left the kitchen. Yick, I bet I'd hurt his feelings. I wanted to explain—but I couldn't exactly *say* I wished he'd find his own friends or go bug Mom instead of me.

Later, as Jess and I were warming up for our second game, I asked her how come she wasn't mad that *my* dad could spend time with us while *her* dad worked day and night.

"Because it's been fun," Jess said. "Plus, my mom says it's *your* dad who's taking all the risks."

I laughed. "At the beach? At the pool? His biggest *risk* is sunburn!"

Jess shrugged. "Well, it's brave to walk out on a job, because maybe they won't let him walk back *in*. My mom says that since computers can do everything so fast now, a bunch of those old jobs won't really exist anymore."

"My dad's job better exist!" I said. "And they better take him back *soon*! I can't stand it much longer. It's like having a big slobbery dog with muddy paws jumping on me all the time!"

I expected Jess to laugh, but she just rolled her eyes.

"Well, *you* always wanted a dog," I muttered.

It was an away game against Channel Two, so they had more fans in the stands than we did—although my dad made as much racket as any eight Channel Two fans put together. And baby Riley, imitating my dad, made more than his share of noise, in spite of Aunt Ann trying to shush him. Their field was in a park with picnic tables and trees. Our field had the *Press Gazette* building and the plaza on one side, and horn-honking, car-alarm-shrieking, exhaust-spewing downtown streets on the others—without a tree in sight. Channel Two's field was certainly nicer to look at, but I figured ours made us tougher.

We won the game by a mile, and we were all jumping around hugging and squealing when Linea (who'd struck out *twice*) suddenly turned to Jess and me with a scowl and said, "I hope your father gets what he deserves!" Then she pranced away tossing her ponytail. I'd never noticed how dorky she looked with her hair poking through her cap like that.

"What's Linea mad about?" I asked Jess. "We won!"

"Which father?" Jess asked me back.

Sometimes Linea was funny, but other times she could be a royal pain—of the bossy, know-it-all variety. She was always on me to choke up on the bat and step into my swing (as if *she* was such a great hitter). And she was forever "helping" me with my fielding too. But what she had against Dad or Uncle Dave, I had no clue.

Maybe she thought Jess and I were twins. People often did. We had the same last name, same brown eyes and blond hair, and we wore the same size. Jess was cuter, though. No one admitted that, but I knew it was true. And she got better grades, despite the fact that I was three weeks and two days older than her and should have been that much smarter.

We'd heard about twins who'd been separated at birth. Years later they're brought together to discover they both like pinky rings, or they both married men with motorcycles, or named their daughters Louise. Jess and I considered ourselves twins separated *before* birth.

"Maybe it's a strike thing," Jess said, watching Linea.

I laughed. "Yeah, like three strikes and you're *out*."

"No," Jess said, "the other strike. Really creepy stuff is happening."

"You always think creepy stuff is happening," I teased.

"Do not!"

"Do too. What about Lamp Ghost?"

Jess shoved me. She hated it when I mentioned Lamp Ghost. But whenever we slept at Gram's, Jess always made me cover it up with a towel. It was just a weird lamp in Gram's loft, but it made Jess really, really nervous.

"I'm serious!" she said. "Someone left a mean note in our mailbox. I heard my mom talking about it on the phone."

"For real?" I asked. "A striker?"

"I guess so."

"What kind of *mean*?" I asked. "Was it like 'You're ugly'? Or like 'I'm gonna cut out your liver and feed it to your cat'?"

Jess frowned. "I don't know. Mom clammed up as soon as she caught me listening."

The thought of someone sneaking up to Jess's mailbox and slipping a nasty note in there icked me out.

We stared at each other. Then I looked past her and saw the boys' team tromping onto the field. Abe saluted me like a soldier. He'd cropped his hair short. It looked like it would feel bristly. I blushed thinking about touching his hair.

I guess Jess caught the salute and the blush, because she said, "Abe?" and her eyes went wide. "He's cute!"

"He's a snob," I said. "Thinks he's so great."

"Well, he *is* great," Jess said, nudging me. "At baseball anyway."

Instead of dropping Dad and me at home after the game, Aunt Ann invited us over for burgers. Riley was thrilled. He'd been hanging on to my dad like a baby chimp all day. I figured it was because he missed his own dad and mine was second best. We called Mom and she brought dessert.

It was strange to see Aunt Ann at the barbecue grill. My uncle had always played that position.

"These are better than Dave's," Dad said, waving his burger around.

"You know what happened after the game?" I asked the adults. "A girl on our team said something to Jess and me about our *father* getting what he *deserves*."

"She must've thought we were sisters," Jess added.

"Do you think it's about your strike?" I asked Dad. But he didn't answer.

"I'm sure it was nothing," Mom said. "Nothing at all."

And everyone just chewed awhile.

After dinner Jess and I went to her room and started setting up a ninety-zillion piece jigsaw puzzle. Riley waddled in, his legs bowed beneath his huge diaper. He snatched a fistful of puzzle pieces and shoved them into his mouth.

"Mom!" Jess and I yelled at once.

My mom came in, scooped up Riley, fished the soggy pieces out of his mouth, and said to me, "Let's go, kiddo."

"Now?" I asked. Usually the grown-ups sat around for ages after dinner.

"How come?" Jess asked.

"Uncle Bill has a union meeting," Mom said, looking embarrassed. "He's dropping us at home on the way."

"Ten minutes?" I begged.

Mom said, "Five."

When she left the room, I said, "Yick!"

And Jess said, "Double yick, Gwen! *Your* dad's going to that meeting to complain about *my* dad. And do you know who else'll probably be there? The guy who left the mean note in our mailbox!"

"Jess," I said, "what should we do?"

"Do?"

"To *fix* it. Write letters to our congressman or something?"

Jess slapped herself on the forehead. "Why didn't I think of that?" she teased. "A letter from us'll end that strike in a tick! And while we're at it, why not add a P.S. to stop world hunger?"

"It was just a thought," I mumbled. Jess always kidded me about my "big ideas," and I usually didn't mind. But this time I really wanted a big idea—something that would keep creeps away from Jess's mailbox and send my dad back to work.

Chapter Three
THUNDER AND LIGHTNING

I WOKE THE next morning to the crash of thunder. The neighbors' tree was flailing around as if trying to beat the lightning out of the sky. Then everything calmed down, leaving a bruise-colored sky full of gloomy rain.

I don't know why Coach Marty bothered to call; it was obvious that practice was canceled.

"Hey, Dad," I said. "Wanna take Jess and me to a movie?"

"Movies cost a fortune," he snapped. "You think I'm made of money? And close that refrigerator door. Electricity costs too, you know."

"Huh?" Dad was suddenly worried about the cost of electricity?

Then, I guess as an apology, he challenged me to a game of Scrabble—knowing I can't resist Scrabble on a rainy day. But when our grandfather clock bonged, Dad jumped to his feet and said he had to get ready for another meeting. We hadn't even finished our game.

It was still raining. I called Jess, but no one answered and the machine wasn't on. I went out to Mom's studio, but she was too busy to talk. She said I could invite Jess over to spend the night, but when I called again, there was still no answer. I was bored to death.

The day dragged.

Dad came home in a foul mood and grumbled something about everyone being jerks. Dinner conversation was nothing but "strike this" and "negotiations that."

Mom asked if we'd all like to go to the riverfront that evening, but Dad said he had to get to the picket line.

"Just as well." Mom shrugged. "I've got a ton of work."

Finally, Jess called. She said her mom would rather we slept there. Uncle Dave wasn't home and she wanted company.

"He's *still* not there?" I asked.

"I guess he has to do a bunch of jobs beside his own—you know, other people's work," Jess answered. I wondered if "other people" meant my dad.

"They haven't missed a day, you know," Jess added.

I was confused. "Who hasn't missed a day of what?"

"The paper." Jess hesitated. I could tell she was embarrassed, but I didn't know why. "The paper hasn't missed a day. Even with all the people out on, well, you know . . . strike, the paper has come out every day."

"So?"

I could hear Jess shrug through the phone. "So nothing. It's just that that's why my dad is always at work, he's . . . you know, getting the newspaper out."

I could tell that Jess was proud of that. I wondered with a twinge what she thought of *my* dad.

When he dropped me at Jess's on his way to the picket line, Dad didn't come in to say hi, even though the rain had stopped. I thought that seemed unfriendly, but maybe he was running late.

Riley was cranky. Aunt Ann said he must be getting a cold or something. She was carrying him around and singing off-key. Jess and I ducked outside to get away from them.

It seemed extra dark in the backyard, with the clouds speeding across an eyelash of moon. The grass was squishy, the air smelled like drowned worms, and the fireflies were blinking. It was like a scene from a science fiction thriller—as if a spaceship was about to materialize out of the mist.

Jess said, "Riley's driving me crazy. You should've seen the clump of hair he pulled out of my head for no reason! I probably have a bald spot!" She rubbed her scalp.

"I bet he misses your dad," I said. I missed Uncle Dave myself. He always greeted me with a "Gimme five—up high!" I'd jump to slap his big palm, then he'd lower his hand and say, "Down low." But he'd pull his hand away before I could catch him, saying, "Too slow!" I'd *never* caught his "down low," although I'd been trying all my life.

"Where were you all day?" I asked Jess.

"Here," she said.

"But I called a million times."

"Our power was out," she said. "Phone, electricity, everything. From the storm." She pointed at the dead streetlights. "Look. Those still haven't recovered."

"So that's why it's so dark," I realized aloud.

Then Aunt Ann's silhouette appeared at the screen door. "Jessica! Gwendolyn! Come inside, girls," she said.

"But, *Mom!*" Jess whined automatically. Then I think we both realized (at the same time) that we'd been called by our full names. That was weird enough to make us obey. So we went inside and straight to Jess's bedroom. We turned on the radio. The Ricky Ronalds show was on. That's the one where people call in to talk about their problems. It always cracks us up.

We were listening and laughing, and imitating Ricky Ronalds (who *always* said "Try once more to risk the right thing"), so we'd only half noticed that the phone was ringing like mad and Aunt Ann was forever answering it.

But then it was ringing nonstop. "Mom must be in the bathroom," Jess said.

We darted for the kitchen, but just as Jess was about to grab the phone, someone whispered, "Don't answer it."

I jumped! It was Aunt Ann. She was right behind us, sitting at the table with Riley on her lap. She half smiled at Jess and me and said, "Let it ring. It's okay. Just some pranksters."

It was as if we were all freeze-framed, like someone had pressed the pause button on the VCR. The phone kept ringing and ringing, and Aunt Ann kept smiling and smiling. Even Riley was quiet—listening. It was eerie.

"What if it's Daddy?" Jess asked in a shaky little voice.

Aunt Ann smiled her strange smile and said, "Maybe tomorrow I'll look into getting an unlisted number."

The phone rang again, jangling every brain cell in my head. I reached out and unplugged it, but then we could hear the other phone still ringing in Aunt Ann and Uncle Dave's room. I ran to unplug that one too, and the ringing stopped dead. The new silence was practically louder than the phone had been.

When I got back to the kitchen, Jess said, "Let's call Gram."

That sounded good to me. But Aunt Ann shook her head and said, "There's nothing Gram could do."

"She could come over," Jess begged. "Be with us."

I agreed completely. No phone would *dare* ring like that if our grandmother were there. I felt better just thinking of her getting out of her big car, marching up the walk, and knocking her one hard knock on the door.

But Aunt Ann said, *"Gone with the Wind?"*

We'd probably watched *Gone with the Wind* fifty times together. And we were always ready to watch it again. Scarlett O'Hara was our hero.

There were a million questions I was dying to ask about the phone calls, but I could tell Aunt Ann didn't want to discuss it. So while she lugged Riley around making double-sure all the doors were locked, I put a bag of popcorn in the microwave and Jess got the video off the shelf. I wished we'd slept at my house. I wished we'd *all* slept at my house—Aunt Ann and Riley too.

We got on Aunt Ann's bed and propped ourselves up with

pillows. Jess pulled the blanket up to her nose, although it was about two hundred degrees in there. Riley was asleep before the opening credits were over.

Uncle Dave still wasn't home when we woke up in the morning. Aunt Ann said he was helping out on the loading docks. I tried to picture him heaving big bundles of papers off the conveyor belts. I wondered if he took off his coat and tie to do that.

We'd gone down to the loading docks on a field trip with our fourth-grade class. Jess and I had thought it was funny that in all our zillions of visits to the paper to see our dads, neither of us had ever before been to the incredibly noisy loading docks or the even noisier ink-smelling pressroom. They'd both felt light-years different from the hush of the carpeted editorial offices.

"My dad helps in all kinds of weird places now," Jess said. Again I wondered if that included *my* dad's office.

Then Dad arrived to drive Jess and me to our third game. He honked instead of coming to the door, although he'd always told me that honking was rude. On our way out my aunt handed Jess a wad of money. "You buy the pizza or whatever after the game this time," she told Jess.

When we got to the field, I saw Linea. I poked Jess and said, "She's not worthy of her *L* name. Maybe we should drop the *L* and call her Nay-ah!" We both giggled because it sounded like a donkey braying. *Nay Ah! Nay Ah!*

"Should we say something?" Jess whispered.

"I don't know," I said. "Like what?"

Jess shrugged.

Then at the end of the first inning Linea got in my face and said, "Your father's such a greed-head. It grosses me out!" She sneered at the stands where Dad was.

"Huh?" It took a second for her words to sink in, and by then Coach Marty was yelling at us to hustle, so I ran to the dugout—and fumed.

Linea was up first. She marched to the plate and swung wild—strike one! Ha! Again—strike two! Hee! Strike three! I cackled while twirling my invisible mustache.

Jess caught my grin and frowned at me.

I still figured Linea had Jess and me mixed up or thought we had the same dad. The strikers may have been acting jerky—making prank calls and leaving mean notes in mailboxes—but as for *greed,* it was management who wouldn't give the workers "Fair PAY! To-DAY!" Right?

Oscar Automotive didn't make a single run. Not one. We creamed them. "No thanks to *her!*" I said to Jess, pointing to Linea. I knew that wasn't very team-spirited, but tough. "She can't bat worth dirt," I added. "How'd she ever make the league?"

"Linea's mom sells advertising for the paper," Jess said. "I asked Vicky."

"So?"

"So nothing. But that means she's on *my* dad's side," Jess said.

"Hmmm," I said. "Then she really did mean *my* dad. *My* dad is so greedy, it grosses her out? Is that weird or what?"

"You mean it would've been *less* weird if it was *my* dad

who grossed her out?" Jess asked. She was kidding, but not completely.

"Well . . ." I sputtered.

"Nice, Gwen," Jess said, squinting at me sideways.

I was going to defend myself, but Coach Marty called us to huddle. He reminded us that we were headed for Springfield the next morning—our first road game of the season! Hooray! All thoughts of Linea and that whole mess flew right out of my head.

We decided on Chinese food for lunch. Dad hardly spoke during the meal—except when Jess and I started fencing with the chopsticks, and he barked, "Girls, act your age!"

The bill came and Jess pulled out her wad of money and plopped it on the table. "My mom said to use this," she said.

Dad looked at the money as if it were a dead rat. "Put that back in your pocket, Jessica," he said in a hard voice.

Jess turned fish-belly pale but didn't reach for the money. "My mom said," she whimpered.

"And *I* said put it away," Dad growled.

Jess took back the money. I could feel the tears wanting to come out of her eyes.

"Da-ad!" I said.

But he shut me up with a warning face.

We walked to the car in silence, Jess stiff beside me. I leaned toward her, but she looked straight ahead.

I wanted to yell at him for being mean to her, but Dad looked ready to explode. So I didn't make a peep. We dropped Jess at her house.

A few blocks later Dad seemed a little calmer, so I asked him why a woman who sells advertising for the paper would be mad at him.

"Because if I had *my* way, she'd be out of work," he said.

"Why?"

"Because selling ads is how the newspaper makes money."

"So?"

Dad sighed. "You really don't get this, do you, Gwen?"

I shrugged.

"We want the strike to hurt. We want it to bring the *Gazette* to its knees—to stop production." He was using a very patient voice, so patient that it sounded *impatient*. "We don't want them to be able to function without us."

I didn't say anything, but I remembered Jess's pride that the paper hadn't missed a day.

"We've asked our advertisers *not* to advertise and we've asked our readers not to buy the paper until our demands have been met. That way management feels our strike where it counts—in their wallet."

Dad honked angrily at a driver who must have cut him off or something. Then he said, "But if our advertisers and readers don't support the strike, and scabs are willing to sneak in and do our jobs for peanuts—what does management need us back for?"

"*Are* there scabs doing your job?" I asked.

"Yeah."

"Are people still buying the paper and buying ads?"

He nodded.

"So you might never go back to work?" I asked as we

drove up our driveway. I caught the words "You mean we'll be *poor*?" before they flew out of my mouth.

"Don't worry," Dad said as we walked in the house. "It'll all work out. But I better get on that picket line just to make sure. You can come. I'm on from seven to ten."

"I didn't know it was scheduled like that," I said.

"It is now. Solidarity's the thing. Can't have a few guys do all the marching while everyone else goes fishing," he said. "So you want to come tonight or not?"

I said "Sure," although I wasn't at all sure of anything right then. Dad went off somewhere. I looked around the kitchen trying to imagine us poor. Would we have to sell the grandfather clock and Mom's other antiques?

"Gwen! Time to pack!" Mom called from her room.

Pack to move? To some miserable shack? I gasped. But then I remembered we were playing Springfield tomorrow! Yes! A trip was *exactly* what I needed!

Road games were my favorite part of summer league. We got to stay in hotels, and it was like one big pajama party with junk food. Plus, no mater how much we all squabbled and picked at one another at home, on the road we were a *team*! Look out, Springfield!

Mom was one of the chaperones this time, which would be okay, but Jess and I got away with more when other moms came. And we all knew that dad chaperones let us stay up later and eat more sweets than any of the moms did. But it was still totally great.

My mom called out things from her list and I ran around gathering them up, excitement jittering in my chest.

"Maybe Dad will take you next time," she said when I came in with my shoes. "Depends."

"On if he's still on strike?" I asked.

"Yes, and on whether I get a regular job or not," Mom said, as if that were perfectly normal.

"You mean a *job*-job?"

"Maybe," Mom said, tucking T-shirts into the suitcase. I froze, my arms full of cleats and flip-flops. "We had no idea the strike would go on so long," she explained.

We're poor, I thought.

Chapter Four
CAVEMEN AND MONSTERS

AT DINNER THE conversation was nothing but strike—again. If I hadn't needed to hold my fork, I would've put my fingers in my ears. The way this new strike-speak had taken over reminded me of the Pig-Latin craze that ripped through sixth grade the year before. Only this code was way less fun.

I tried to concentrate on twirling my spaghetti while Mom rambled on. "Gwen, do you understand the implications of the typographers union bargaining collectively with the Teamsters and the pressmen?"

I shrugged, wondering if Abe would be at the picket line that night. Wondering too if he was just a friendly-to-everyone kind of guy or if he was being especially friendly to me. The thought made me nervous, so I tried to switch my attention to Dad.

He was looking at me and saying, "The guild and the electricians union have negotiated individually and are settling along with the blah, blah, blah bargaining committee . . . labor relations . . . blah . . ." Or something like that.

I thought of the opening scene in *Gone with the Wind,* when Scarlett doesn't want to hear another word about that "boring old war." I wished I could just say "Fiddle-dee-dee!" like she did, and that Mom and Dad would instantly change the subject to something more jolly. I tried to remember what we used to talk about at dinner. I was sure Dad never used to be so dull.

But before the strike Dad wasn't usually home in time to eat with us. Sometimes Mom and I would make one heaping dish of pasta and go at it together with two forks. That seemed awfully long ago, I thought, looking at our three separate plates.

When Dad *did* make it home for dinner (in the old days), he'd throw his necktie over his shoulder so he wouldn't spill food on it, and he'd tell us funny stories about his day. Back then Mom would joke that she wanted him to sit in the window so the neighbors could see that she really did have a husband.

Well, the neighbors sure knew that now! Dad was the most at-home, around-the-house husband on the whole block.

After dinner Mom said, "I don't know why you need to go picket with Dad again, Gwen. You've been there. You've seen it." She cracked a crooked smile. "It's not like you're fascinated with the political situation."

I shrugged. "It's fun," I said. "Some of my friends go." I forced myself not to blush when I thought of Abe, and added, "They've got free donuts."

Mom rolled her eyes, then turned to Dad. "Don't forget, she has a seven a.m. bus tomorrow, so no stopping for snacks on the way home tonight."

"No need for snacks," he said. "Like Gwen said, there're plenty of donuts."

In the car I tried to act interested in Dad's strike, since that was all he cared about these days. I asked him why Aunt Ann was getting mean phone calls.

He seemed surprised.

"Didn't Uncle Dave tell you about it?" I asked.

"I haven't talked to him," Dad said.

"Not at *all*?" I gasped.

"It would look bad," he said. "People might think we're swapping secrets."

When I finally recovered my ability to breathe, I said, "Whoever's calling Aunt Ann is on *your* side, right?"

"Slimy little creeps make us all look bad," Dad said. "Same slimeballs who did that to the Chevy dealer."

"Did what?" I asked, already sorry I'd brought the whole thing up.

"Gwen, where've you been? That's all anyone's been talking about!"

"Well, excuse me," I mumbled. "*Some* of us aren't thinking about your strike every second." And though I doubted I wanted to hear the answer, I asked, "What did they do to the Chevy dealer?"

"Dumped oil paint on the new cars in his lot. Slashed some tires. They hoped it would discourage him from continuing to advertise in the scab paper."

"Discourage him? You mean *scare* him!" I said, my voice squeaking.

"Gwen, these are the tools of the powerless," Dad said. "Management has all the big guns: They've got the building, the presses, the fancy lawyers. They can just tilt back in their comfy chairs and happily starve us. On the other hand, we've got nothing—and no choice but to fight back like cavemen, like terrorists."

Dad glanced at me, then quickly added, "That is, *some* strikers think violence and vandalism are our only options. They're wrong, of course."

The sun set in war-movie colors, as if a village were burning in the distance. I pictured sentries posted in the *Press Gazette* penthouse, scanning the plaza in case we started slinging arrows or catapulting boulders.

I spotted Vicky at the same time she saw me, and we moved toward each other like magnets. "Who are ya bunking with in Springfield?" I asked her.

Vicky shrugged. "I'll see when we get there," she said.

I always bunked with Jess, so it had never occurred to me to wonder how anyone else picked partners.

Vicky leaned close and whispered, "Liza snores. I mean *really* snores!" Then she cracked up and so did I.

We wandered around, pigging out on donuts and talking about the girls on our team. I wondered why I'd never really noticed how fun Vicky was—and nice.

I felt a tap on my shoulder and spun around (with my mouth full!) to find Abe grinning down at me. Boy, was he tall!

"Donuts again?" he said.

I swallowed quickly, brushing frantically at my face and hoping I wasn't covered with crumbs. Vicky held her donut high and exclaimed, "Union soul food! Strike fuel!"

Abe laughed. "So, did you guys hear what happened at our game?" he asked.

"You lost?" I teased.

"Sort of," he said. "But actually—" Then there was a sudden uproar. Yelling. "It's the shift change," Abe said, craning his neck toward the building entrance.

I tried to see over all the heads but only caught glimpses of people scurrying out of the *Press Gazette* building in tight bunches. I guessed they were scabs, or management like Uncle Dave. Whoever they were, they were running hunched, as if against an icy wind. But it was hot out and the air was still.

The picketers hollered at them as they hurried by. I couldn't tell what they were saying (because they all roared over one another), but the meanness was crystal clear.

Then there was more commotion, this time at the parking lot. A bunch of strikers were racing for a little red Volkswagen that was coming out through the gate. They were yelling and shaking their fists, casting long shadows in the glare of the parking lot lights.

The Volkswagen sped up, but two men jumped in front of it. The driver slammed on the brakes and the car lurched to a stop. It honked and honked, sounding like a baby animal cut off from its herd. The mob of strikers pushed closer, surrounding it. Then they started hammering the car with their fists! In their shadows they looked like killers—cavemen slaughtering their prey.

Dad and Coach Marty grabbed Vicky, Abe, and me, and pulled us away. But not before I saw the Volkswagen's red roof begin to rock. The strikers were shoving the car. The driver probably wanted to floor it and mow them all down. I sure would have! But the Volkswagen just stayed frozen—honking.

Finally the police appeared with their clubs out, and the bullies ran off. The car sped away like a shot. That's when I realized I'd been screaming and that Dad was holding me so tight, he was practically choking me.

"The poor guy in that car!" I cried.

"That wasn't a guy," Vicky yelled. "That was Linea's mom! Mrs. Richardson!"

The next thing I knew, Dad was carrying me, hurrying to our car. He buckled my seat belt for me and said, "I'll start looking for another job tomorrow morning. I'm out of here!"

He kept talking, but I didn't listen. I was thinking how terrified Linea's mom must've been. Trapped in her tiny car, an angry mob pressing in on her. I imagined being alone in there. Hearing them. Feeling the whole car shake. Seeing nothing out the windshield but hate. In spite of the hot, muggy night, I was shivering.

Then at home my parents crowded in on either side of me on the couch while Dad told Mom about it. I was so ashamed of him and his strikers that I couldn't even look at him.

I stood up, my legs wobbling, and managed to say, "All this time I thought the other side was the bad guys." Then I went to my room and crawled under the blankets with all my clothes on.

Mom came in and sat on the edge of my bed. "There's no excuse for how those people acted," she began. "But don't blame your dad. Everyone, including him, expected this to be a short strike, with both sides negotiating in good faith and settling quickly. Unfortunately, it didn't go that way."

I just stared at the goose bumps on my arm while Mom droned. "I work, and Dad and I had some money saved. But some of the folks who went crazy out there don't have any income now. They're so scared, they went nuts."

"You just said there was no excuse for how they acted," I said. "So how come you're making excuses?"

Just then the phone rang and Dad yelled, "Gwen, it's Jess." I left Mom sitting there and pulled the blankets with me to the phone.

"Did you see the news?" Jess shrieked as soon as I'd said hello. *"Did you?"*

"No," I said.

"You've *got* to turn on your TV," she said. "You won't be-lieve it!" Then she described the Volkswagen scene. I hadn't noticed a news crew there, but there must've been. I pulled the blankets tighter around me.

"I was there," I admitted, shivering with shame. But I guess I spoke too quietly, because Jess said, "Huh?"

"I was there," I repeated, louder.

"You were *there*? On the plaza? When those . . . those . . . *animals* attacked that car? Wow! Was that insane or what? Those aren't people! They're *monsters*! Worse than monsters! Can you believe the police didn't even arrest them? They let those animals just walk away!"

I didn't know how to respond but I managed a grunt. Jess didn't notice. She went on to say, "No one has any idea yet whose car that was, but can you *imagine* being him?"

"It was Nay-ah's mom," I said quietly.

"*What?* Are you *sure*?" Jess shrieked.

"Pretty sure," I said. Jess didn't answer, so I said, "Jess?" And again: "Jess?" But the line was dead. Had she pushed the wrong button by mistake or purposely hung up on me?

I started to call her back—but to say what? I wrapped my-self tight in my blankets, crept to my room, and crawled into bed again.

Maybe I just dreamed Mom's voice getting shrill in the liv-ing room, saying, "I *told* you a picket line was no place for a young girl, Bill! But did you listen to me? Do you *ever* listen to me?"

Chapter Five
SPRINGFIELD OR BUST

MY ALARM WENT off in the dark, and all the weirdness of the day before came back to me with the first trace of light. The rocking Volkswagen, Jess hanging up on me, Mom mad at Dad, possible poverty. I tried to shove it to the back of my brain, behind the excitement of a road game. I told myself that everything would be okay once we got on the bus and out of town.

I hauled my duffel bag through thick gray fog to the car. Our front yard was like an island in a cloud, with the world disappearing in all directions. I was foggy on the inside too—a mix of grogginess, anticipation, and dread. Minus the dread,

I recognized the feeling from last summer and the summers before: It was my morning-of-a-road game mood.

As we drove, the fog shredded into wisps that slid through the beams of our headlights, and by the time Mom and I got to Jess's, the sun was up and the day was completely clear.

Jess kissed Aunt Ann and baby Riley good-bye, threw her stuff in the trunk with mine, and got in the backseat next to me. The first thing out of her mouth was: "Linea says we're lucky we're even going!"

"Linea?" I gasped, remembering again the dead phone in my hand last night. "You called *Nay-ah*?"

Jess nodded as if it was no big deal. "She told me that at the boys' game yesterday some parents got into a shouting match. Almost a fistfight! They canceled their next game and they're talking about suspending the boys' whole season until the strike is settled!"

"No!" I shrieked.

"Yes!"

"That must be what Abe was going to say," I said.

"Abe?" Jess's eyes got bigger.

Then Mom said, "The bus is late." We'd arrived at the field.

Coach Marty and some moms rushed up to us as we got out of our car. "Sorry you showed up for nothing," Coach Marty said. "I've canceled Springfield."

I felt like I'd been slapped. *"What?"* Jess and I wailed.

"There's too much tension on the team," Coach Marty explained. "I can't risk taking it on the road."

"Good!" my mother said.

My head jerked to look at her. "Good?"

"I'm sure that's the best decision," Liza's mom agreed. "I couldn't sleep last night, worrying about this trip."

"But . . . but . . . that's all backwards!" I sputtered. "The trouble is *here*, not in Springfield!"

Liza's mom patted my head as if I were a pet—too dumb to understand. I wanted to slug her. Slug all of them!

"It feels wrong to see our girls with PRESS GAZETTE stamped on their shirts at a time like this," Marsha's mom said, and the other grown-ups nodded as if that made sense.

I turned to Jess, but she was gone—way across the parking lot. With Linea. That's when I noticed that everyone had separated into two groups. The few people around me were all ones I'd seen at the picket line. The girls and parents over where Jess stood must've been management. The world had gone mad! Trips canceled, people dividing into enemy camps . . . *Yick!*

I stomped over to where Vicky, Marsha, and Liza (the girls on "my" side) were sitting.

"We have to fight this!" I said to them.

Vicky snorted. "How? Hijack a bus to Springfield? Pitch tents on their field till game time?"

I couldn't believe that she, of all people, was joking about this. It was *her* dad who'd canceled our trip. "I'm serious," I said. "We have to *do* something!"

"It's hopeless," Marsha grumbled, and I saw her eyes tear up. Liza looked near tears too.

"It's just a *newspaper!*" Vicky said. "I mean, I miss the

comics, and it's a drag having to line my bird's cage with toilet paper . . . but still—what's the big stink about a *newspaper?*"

Then Mom came over and told me to get Jess so we could go home. Jess was only a few yards away—about the distance from home plate to first—but I couldn't move.

Trina Johnson and her mother pulled up, and Coach Marty rushed over to tell them the horrid news. I couldn't hear Coach Marty, but I sure heard Trina's mom. "This is an outrage!" she hollered. "You people will stop at *nothing* to ruin our lives, will you?"

Coach Marty said something else, and Trina ducked behind her mom. Mrs. Johnson yelled, "Haven't you people done enough damage without taking it out on the *children?*"

Yes! I thought. At least *one* grown-up understands! I wanted to cheer: "You tell 'em, Mrs. Johnson!" But she didn't see my smile as she marched toward the management crowd with Trina close on her heels.

"Gwen," Mom snapped, "I asked you to get Jess. We're leaving."

"I'll come with you," Vicky offered.

"No, that's silly," I said, embarrassed that she knew what I was thinking.

"That's okay," Vicky said. "I don't mind being silly."

I didn't thank her, although I wanted to. "I feel like we're scouts crossing enemy lines," I whispered.

"Infiltrators!" Vicky added, giggling.

"And they've got my cousin hostage!"

Vicky didn't say so, but I bet she was thinking that Jess had gone willingly. After all, Jess was one of *them!*

We made it there and back without incident, though. We didn't have to fight anyone off or pull Jess from the opposition's clutches. I said, "Jess, we gotta go," and she said, "Okay." But none of the other girls spoke to us, and nobody smiled.

In the car Jess said, "Leave it to the boys to screw things up for everyone!"

I wondered if Jess was blaming the boys so she wouldn't have to blame her own dad. I knew the strike wasn't *all* Uncle Dave's fault, but if his side would just stop being so greedy, we'd be on our way to Springfield.

"I'm so sorry, girls," Mom said as she drove. "I know how much you were looking forward to this trip."

"If she's so sorry," I muttered to Jess, "why'd she let it happen?"

"Why'd your *dad* and them have to walk out in the first place?" Jess answered. I knew she couldn't really mean that it was entirely the strikers' fault, so I didn't object. And they *were* the ones who started it. But they walked out for good reason—because they were being cheated, right?

It seemed to me that both of our dads were wrong, and Coach Marty, and my mom . . . all the so-called "grownups" were guilty. But how could everybody be wrong? My thoughts were swimming.

Then Jess picked up her invisible phone. "Hello," she whispered.

"Hello. Who's this?" I whispered back.

"The President of the U.S. of A."

"Hello, ma'am. What can I do for you?"

"End the strike," Jess said. "And that's an order."

"Yes, ma'am," I said, wishing I could. We hung up, and rode the rest of the way to Jess's house looking out separate windows.

Aunt Ann didn't seem surprised to see us pull up. The moms went inside and Jess and I stood on her front lawn feeling lost. She tossed me a ball, starting a slow, sad game of catch.

"We're not supposed to be here!" she wailed. "Don't you think it knocks the universe off orbit when people aren't where they belong?"

I nodded, glumly lobbing her the ball.

"Like there's a master plan for who's supposed to be where," Jess said, "and if people mess with it, the solar system goes flooey. Then you get swarms of killer bees or tidal waves or something."

"What are we going to do with the next two days?" I asked, because that's how long we'd planned to be in Springfield.

"I'm going swimming with Linea tomorrow," Jess said, all casual and innocent.

I missed her throw. *"What?"*

Jess shrugged. "She invited me."

"When?"

"Tomorrow."

"No, I mean when did she invite you?"

"Just now, at the field," Jess said, sounding annoyed.

She was annoyed? How about *me*? Jess was suddenly pals with the girl who called my dad names? Killer bees and tidal waves would be nothing compared to this!

"You're *friends*? With *Nay-ah*?" I brayed. "The Nay-ah who called your very own uncle a greed-head?"

"Gwen, for Pete's sake, she's on our *team!*" Jess said. "And she won't say stuff like that anymore. I asked her not to bug you."

"Gee, thanks," I said sarcastically.

Jess sighed. "She was just upset," she said. "And who wouldn't be? Strikers scream and swear at her mom every single day as she goes in and out of work. And then the thing with the car! Her mom was a total wreck. But Linea doesn't blame your dad *personally*."

"Well, that's big of her," I mumbled.

Jess rolled her eyes. "Get over it, Gwen!"

I threw her a fastball. She ducked. "Sorry," I lied.

When we went inside to get a drink, my aunt and my mom got quiet and stayed quiet, which was weird. Then Mom stood up and said, "Let's go, kiddo." She hugged Aunt Ann good-bye, which was also weird; Mom and Aunt Ann never hug. But with everything else going wacko in my life, the moms were just one more wack.

I was so deep in my own misery that I hadn't noticed how bone-quiet it was in the car until Mom said, "Gwen, honey, I've got something to tell you." But then she was silent for another block and a half.

Finally she cleared her throat and said, "It seems that the newspaper was very *disappointed* that Marty canceled the Springfield trip. They want the team to go forward with the season."

"Good!" I said.

"So," Mom continued as if I hadn't spoken, "they're bringing in a new coach."

"What?" I shrieked. "They fired Coach Marty?"

"Not exactly." She sighed. "He sort of resigned."

"We're going to Springfield without him?"

Mom sighed again. "It's too late for Springfield, but they *are* going ahead with the rest of the games."

"Without Coach Marty? No way!" I said. "He's our *coach!*"

"Nonetheless, Marty's leaving the team. And so is Vicky, of course. Marsha and Liza are too."

I couldn't breathe. "What are you *talking* about?" I gasped.

"Gwen, did you hear what Dora Johnson said to Marty about 'you people'? Something like, 'You people ruin everything'?"

"Yeah, so?"

"Who do you think she meant? Who do you think 'you people' are?" Mom said as she pulled up our driveway. "It's your decision," she added.

Dad saw us arrive and came out to meet us. "You told her?" he asked Mom.

"Told me *what?*" I yelled. "I don't get it! What are you telling me?"

"There're other leagues," Dad said. "I'm sure there are plenty of teams who'd be thrilled to get their mitts on you."

"I have a team!" I cried.

We somehow made it up the walk, through the front door, and into the kitchen. "I gotta call Jess," I said.

"Wait a bit," Mom said, putting her hand on my shoulder. "Try to think this through first."

I shrugged her hand off and grabbed the phone, waving her out of the room. Jess answered, knowing it was me. "Gwen?"

I said, "Is this insane or what?"

"Worse than insane!" Jess shrieked.

"My parents *say* it's up to me—but they want to pull me off the team," I told her.

"No!"

"Yes! And Coach Marty's off. Vicky, Marsha, and Liza are too."

"I know!"

"*All* the strikers' kids but *ME.* Jess, what should we do?"

"We?" Jess asked.

"Well, we're going to stay, right?"

"*I* am," Jess said, getting quiet. "My side isn't talking about quitting."

I suddenly felt chilled. "*Your* side?" I asked.

"Well, you know what I mean," she said, even quieter. "The *team* is still there."

"Without Coach Marty?" I said angrily. "Or Vicky or Liza or Marsha?" I almost said "Without me," but I was afraid that saying it would make it true. "Maybe it's a team, but it's not the *same* team!"

Jess didn't say anything.

I said, "I gotta go."

"Talk to you later," she answered in a tiny voice.

I ducked out the front door and down the drive. I didn't

see any of the houses or notice any neighbors. I just walked, my thoughts in a tangle.

After a while a car pulled up beside me. I glanced over. It was Mom.

"You didn't tell me where you were going," she said, sounding scared.

"I'm not going anywhere," I said.

"Well, get in. It's time for lunch."

I didn't want lunch. I didn't want a ride home. I wanted to be on my way to Springfield to play ball. I wanted to wake up and realize this whole mess had just been a nightmare.

"I'm not hungry," I said.

"Come on, Gwen," Mom said stiffly. "I don't want you out here alone like this."

"Alone like what? Mom, it's the middle of the day."

She checked her rearview mirror and darted looks down the street. "Please get in the car, Gwendolyn," she said, reminding me of when Aunt Ann called Jess and me inside on the night of the phone calls. What were the moms scared of? Mugging? Kidnapping?

But that would mean Mom was worried about Aunt Ann's side doing the kidnapping and Aunt Ann was worried about Mom's. Could everyone have gone so completely crazy?

Mom tried to smile at me but failed.

I got in and slumped against the car door.

I knew she was being overly dramatic, but on the short ride home I couldn't help scanning the streets, although I had no idea what I was looking for.

• • •

That night at dinner, everyone was quiet, especially Dad.

"Do they *want* me to quit?" I asked, breaking the silence.

"Has anyone *said* they want me off the team?"

"No, of course not," Mom answered.

"So it's just *your* idea? You two want me to quit?"

"We don't *want* you to," Mom said. "But we do think it would be best."

I poked at my macaroni and cheese. "Well, I'm not quitting," I told them.

"You don't have to decide right now," Mom said.

"Too late. I've decided."

"Don't forget, the *Press Gazette* sponsors that team," she said, as if anyone had let me forget that for one microsecond.

"So?" I yelled. "That has nothing to do with me! I'm not on your side or *any* side of this stupid strike!"

It wasn't like my dad to just sit there, but he didn't say a thing. He just kept eating as if he were alone in the room.

"Gwen," Mom said, "sometimes fate picks what side we're on. We're born an untouchable in India. A slave on a plantation. A Jew in Poland during Nazi occupation. Sometimes events larger than ourselves determine our lives."

"But you're the one who says I can be whatever I want to be! Remember?"

Mom sighed. "Dad didn't want to go on strike, you know."

If she could talk about him as if he weren't there, so could I. "If *he* didn't think it was right, he should've said no. You always tell *me* to do what I think is right!"

"It's not that simple," Mom said, shooting a glance at my

silent father. "Dad had to pick the lesser of two evils. He happened to be well-paid, but others in his union were not. If he'd thought only of himself and crossed the picket line, it would've undermined what everyone else was trying to accomplish."

I shoved my plate away. "And what does pulling me from my team *accomplish*? Who does it help? No one! It just hurts me and my team!"

My father carefully dabbed his lips with his napkin. My mother sighed.

Vicky called and said, "Strike two!" as her hello.

I was amazed that she was still joking.

"Maybe for strike three," she went on, "they'll *strike* us on the bean with an ax! Or lightning will *strike*. And isn't it called an air *strike* when they drop bombs from planes?"

"I hate the word," I said, "every which way."

"Then let's *strike* it from the record!"

Vicky laughed—but I couldn't.

Then she asked if I wanted to go to strike headquarters with her tomorrow. I had no idea what she meant, so she explained that strike headquarters was where families went to hang out. "I like to help with the babies," she said.

Yick—strikers and their babies. I didn't want anything to do with that whole mess.

"There are some cute guys there too," Vicky added. "Abe and his friends sometimes drop by."

That caught me off guard. I told her my brain was still rattled from today's shock and I'd have to talk to her tomorrow.

I hung up and went to my room.

The sun was setting fast and everything was dimming. Years of team pictures faded into my bedroom wall, taking Jess and me with them. I let my eyes close, darkening the dark, and put the pillow over my head.

Chapter Six
THE SUMMIT MEETING

THE ROAR OF the lawn mower woke me. I opened my eyes and the first thing I saw was my duffel bag. It was a steep down-hill slide from there—remembering that I was supposed to be in Springfield and that my parents thought I should quit the team. It was only eight a.m. and the day already stunk.

I dragged myself to the kitchen and poured a bowl of ce-real. The phone rang and I answered with my mouth full.

"Is Gwen home?" Vicky asked.

"It's me," I said.

"Really? Are you tied up and gagged or something? Grunt once if I should call 911."

"Eating," I said with a laugh.

Dad came in the side door. He was sweat-streaked, with grass stuck all over his legs. *He'd* been mowing the lawn? Himself? What happened to the gardeners, I wondered. Then it hit me like a snowball: We couldn't afford gardeners anymore.

I turned my attention back to Vicky, who was saying, "My dad's gonna work the phone bank at headquarters."

"The what?"

"It's a strike hot line for people with questions," she said. "So, you wanna come with me today or not?"

"I guess so," I said. Then I hung up and watched Dad chug down glass after glass of water. He spotted me and made he-man muscles.

"Might as well cancel my gym membership," he said.

It was sort of a joke, so I sort of smiled.

As I finished my breakfast, I thought about Jess. She was going swimming with Nay-ah today. They'd probably talk about what *monsters* my dad and the other strikers were. I wondered what Jess would think of my going to strike "headquarters." Yick—why did it have to sound so *military*?

And at first glance it *did* look armyish: a giant warehouse with an American flag and a gray metal desk right inside the door. The room was ugly but air-conditioned, which felt wonderful.

Coach Marty went straight for the tables with phones, TVs, and radios. A few people were sitting there wearing headphones and scribbling. The command post, I thought. But Vicky explained that they were monitoring strike coverage in the media. "To see if anyone's saying bad stuff about us," she said. "And to see whose side the press is on."

I knew I should pretend to be interested, ask questions or something—but I didn't. Instead, I looked around. This was one strange military base! It seemed to double as a day care center, complete with cribs and banged-up old toys. And it was a rec room too (thank goodness!) with a Ping-Pong table and a collection of balls in a big wire basket.

A wide-eyed little girl came right up to me, shoved the book *Ferdinand* in my face, and squeaked, "Reading me?"

I turned to grab Vicky, but she was being handed a very newborn-looking baby, the pink kind of the wobbly-head-on-a-noodle-neck variety. I decided I'd much rather read than be responsible for that!

I sat down and opened the book, and instantly all kinds of kids came scurrying over to listen. I tried out silly voices and did my best. I even started enjoying myself.

Toward the end of the book I looked up and saw Abe and two other guys walk in the door. I'm sure my voice squeaked.

Abe had a guitar.

My mouth kept reading, but my brain was no longer paying a lick of attention to the story. I heard Abe tuning up. When I said "The end" and closed the book, all the kids ran to him.

Abe strummed a few chords and said, "This is a Woody Guthrie song called 'The Union Maid.'" He was nodding his head and tapping his foot in time. "Here comes the first verse, two, three." Then he started singing. His voice cracked a little at the end of each line, which was kind of sweet.

Then he stopped and said, "This here's the chorus. You're gonna sing this part with me, so listen up. Ready?"

The kids yelled, "Ready!" I could tell they loved him.

Vicky nudged me and whispered, "You're drooling."

I felt myself turn every color in the rainbow. *"I am not!"* I growled, but she just grinned. I couldn't hear the rest of Abe's song because my pulse was jack-hammering in my ears.

After that I tried to keep busy with the little kids, but I wasn't sure what to do with them. I imitated Vicky. She made faces at babies and rolled a ball back and forth with the toddlers, so I did too.

Mostly, I made a point of *not* looking at Abe. But just as we were leaving, he popped up in front of me, grinning his head off. "What are *you* smiling about?" I asked him, pretending to be mad. "That fight at your game got my entire team benched and our Springfield trip canceled! And now Coach Marty quit and the whole thing has gone wacko!"

Abe threw up his hands. "Don't shoot!" he said comically. "It wasn't me, I swear!"

I changed the subject as we moved out into the blasting heat. "So, your song about the union maid," I said. "Was she a maid, like the maiden in the union? Or was she a maid like the kind who sweeps up and cleans the bathrooms?"

Abe threw back his head and howled as if that was hilarious. (I hadn't been joking.) Then he hopped on a blue bicycle and rode off with his guitar slung across his back—still laughing.

• • •

When I got home, Mom told me we'd been summoned to Gram's for dinner.

"Summoned?" I asked.

"Well, it was sure stronger than an invitation," Mom said. "And Aunt Ann says Gram called them too. I think it's Gram's idea of a summit meeting."

"Are Dad and Uncle Dave coming?"

"Apparently so," Mom said. "I don't think anyone was given a choice." She laughed, and that's when I realized there hadn't been much laughter around the house lately. "If anyone could settle this strike," Mom said, "it would be your grandmother. I wish *she* was at the bargaining table."

"But I thought Dad was quitting the strike," I said. "I thought he was going to forget the whole thing!"

Mom looked at me like I was nuts. "He can't just walk away, Gwen."

I pictured a scene from a late-night movie I'd watched recently—a posse hunting down a deserter and dragging him before a firing squad. Were there bounty hunters to track strike deserters? But I shook the thought out of my head, telling myself that *couldn't* be what Mom meant.

My parents collected old stuff, and Jess's house was full of antiques too. But Gram's condo was super-modern and I loved going there. The only thing I didn't love was Gram's cooking. Mom said her food was lousy because she only bought ready-made frozen stuff to nuke in her microwave. But Dad thought the microwave was the best thing that ever happened to Gram's cooking. He said that when he and Uncle Dave were kids, the smoke alarm was their dinner bell because Gram burnt everything.

I saw Gram's newspaper lying in her driveway, but when I bent to get it, Dad yelled, "Don't touch that!" as if it were a bomb.

Then the door flew open and Gram filled the doorway. Jess and her family showed up right behind us. Gram plucked Riley out of Aunt Ann's arms and whisked him away to the kitchen.

Uncle Dave dropped Gram's newspaper on a chair and turned to me. "Gimme five," he said. "Up high!" I slapped him five. "Down low! Too slow!" We both laughed. I'd missed *again,* but it felt great.

Then he stuck his hand out at my dad and said. "Hey, Bill, how ya doin'?"

Dad smiled, shook Uncle Dave's hand, and said, "Great. How's tricks?"

But that was all wrong!! When the dads met, they *always* pretended to punch each other like boxers! I wanted to yell "Stop that! Do it over right!" But no one else seemed alarmed that the dads weren't slugging each other. And at least the moms were acting normal.

Jess and I raced up the stairs to the loft and took a flying leap past Lamp Ghost, landing on Gram's huge bed.

"I'm starved," Jess said. "I hope Gram's making something edible."

I laughed. "I had a P.B. and J. before we left, just in case."

"I meant to," Jess wailed, "but there wasn't time."

My spine went stiff. "Because you were swimming with *Nay-ah* all day?" I asked.

"No, because I was helping Mom paint the bathroom," Jess said, sounding cranky. "Are you going to snip at me about Linea all night?"

"I'm not snipping!" I said. "I just asked—"

"You are *too* snipping. I'm trying to be a good sport about it, but really, Gwen, this jealousy is getting *loony.*"

"*Jealousy?*" I spat. "This has nothing to do with jealousy. You've made friends with my enemy! You're a traitor!"

"Traitor? Enemy?" Jess scoffed. "This isn't a *war,* Gwen."

"And you think *you're* being a good sport?" I shrieked. "Who hung up on who?" We were sitting on opposite ends of Gram's bed by then, glaring at each other.

"What? When?"

"After *Nay-ah's* mother's car thing."

"First of all, stop calling her that! And second, I never hung up on you."

"Did too!"

"Well gimme a break, Gwen, Linea's mom had just been attacked. Anyone would have wanted to call and see how she was." Then Jess squinted at me and said, "*You* didn't call, did you? Those *animals* viciously attack the mother of one of your teammates and you were so busy being jealous, you didn't even call her!"

"Who're you calling *animals?*" I said, getting hot.

"I'm calling those *animals* animals!"

"We aren't animals!" I yelled.

"You? Who said anything about *you?*" Jess yelled back.

"You did! You called me an animal."

"Oh, for Pete's sake, Gwen. I meant the people who attacked Mrs. Richardson's car!"

"We didn't *attack* it. We just rocked it a little." Then I realized what I said, but I was so mad that I didn't take it back.

Jess gaped at me. Then in a very quiet voice she said, "Did you say *we?*"

I shrugged.

"You were part of that?" she asked, her eyes bugging with horror. "You and Uncle Bill?" I watched her swallow as if her throat were choked with dust. "When you said you were *there,* I didn't think you meant . . ."

I folded my arms and didn't answer. My heart was hammering like mad but I was trying to act cool.

Jess's eyes got even bigger. Then she slid off the bed and backed away. At the head of the stairs she turned and ran down.

I stayed exactly where I was, staring dumbly at Lamp Ghost. But when my heartbeat and breathing were more or less normal, I made myself go downstairs too.

Jess and her family sat on one side of Gram's long glass table. My parents and I sat on the other. Gram, of course, sat at the head. I was tied in a fierce knot—hating Jess for what she'd made me say. I couldn't look at her. I couldn't eat.

And I couldn't pay attention to the conversation at first. Then I gradually noticed that the adults were using normal voices to say weird things—like how hot it was yesterday and today and how it would probably be just as hot tomorrow. My family never used to talk about the weather. Who were these people?

Then Uncle Dave complimented Gram's food and all the other grown-ups agreed, although it was the same limp, overzapped stuff she always served us. They went dish by dish.

"Good corn!"

"Great rolls!"

"Love these potatoes!"

I bet Jess was getting creeped out too—but who cared what Jess thought? She'd gone as wacko as the rest of them.

Only Gram seemed like herself, and she wasn't falling for the compliments. She was scowling, and when Mom praised her chicken, she said, "That's enough! We've *thoroughly* discussed the food and the weather. Now can we please move on?"

No one answered.

Gram looked from one of her sons to the other. "What are you going to do about this strike, boys?" she asked.

"Now, Ma, you know we can't talk about it," my dad said.

"I told you that on the phone," Uncle Dave added.

"This room isn't bugged," Gram said. "No one outside of the family will ever know what we discuss here."

"You don't think they know we're brothers?" Dad asked. "You don't think everyone on both sides is watching us for slipups?"

"Baloney!" Gram said. Then she leaned hard on the table and said. "What do you think Poppa would do if he were alive?"

"I think he'd ask what's for dessert," Dad said.

Uncle Dave nodded and smiled.

My grandfather had worked at the *Press Gazette* too, long ago. I didn't remember him; he died when I was really little. Jess said she remembered the feel of his scratchy beard, but I didn't see how she could.

Gram stood up. "Your poppa would be outraged!" she spat.

She put her fists on her wide hips and glared down at her sons. Then she turned and marched into the kitchen. Everyone sat listening to her banging around in there.

Uncle Dave put the salt shaker perfectly in line with the pepper shaker and napkin holder. My father folded and refolded his napkin. The moms sat blankly with their hands in their laps. I didn't look at Jess.

Finally Gram brought out the pie and said, "It's time to cut the nonsense."

My uncle said, "The *nonsense*? I thought it was a pie."

Dad tried to laugh, but no one else did.

"I'm serious, boys," Gram said, her voice low and threatening.

"Sorry, Ma," Uncle Dave said quietly. "We're here to talk about weather and sports."

Dad snorted. "Nope, not sports," he said, pointing his fork at me, then Jess. "Even sports has become a forbidden topic."

Gram cut the pie with stabs of anger. Deep red raspberry goo oozed out as if from a wound. "I cannot allow this strike to tear my family apart!" she said. "Do you hear me?"

Usually I liked the Fountain of Youth and got a kick out of it when Gram yelled at the dads as if they were kids, but tonight it felt bad.

No one spoke. Gram slammed the knife down on the

table. Then she sat heavily in her chair and sighed a gigantic rattly sigh. She put her head in her hands, making my neck prickle. It wasn't like Gram to give up. It wasn't like Gram to lose. It wasn't *at all* like Gram to put her head in her hands and sigh.

I wanted to yell "SOMEONE MAKE THIS BETTER!" I looked around at the grown-ups, waiting for one of them to *fix* this!

But they couldn't, wouldn't—didn't.

No one was in charge here. Everything was out of control. It gave me a strange, bottomless feeling, as if the floor had turned to mush. As if we were careening downhill—picking up speed. The adults had no more of a handle on this than we kids did.

"I gotta get back to work," my uncle said. Then he tossed his napkin on the table and got to his feet.

The rest of us got up to go too. Nobody was in the mood for pie.

I went over to Gram and gave her a squeeze good-bye, then followed my parents out. As Gram's door closed, I felt it shut me off from life as it had always been. I was outside now, alone with the moon, the crickets, and these powerless strangers my parents had become.

Chapter Seven
THE HATE PLAGUE

IT WAS QUIET all the way home from Gram's. When we pulled up our driveway, Dad didn't cut the engine. "Good night, ladies," he said. "I gotta get to the line."

"I thought you quit," I said.

He laughed a not-funny laugh and said, "Wouldn't *that* look great? First have dinner with Dave, then not show up at the picket line."

"Wouldn't that look great to *who*?" I asked.

Mom opened her car door and said, "No one. Come on, Gwen. Let's go."

"Are people watching us?" I asked, looking at the spiky shadows cast by the streetlight.

"Everyone is watching us," Dad said at the same time as Mom said, "*No one's* watching us!" She glared at Dad and said, "For heaven's sake, Bill! Can't you think before you open your mouth?" Then she got out and slammed her car door. *Wham!*

I felt my chest fill with panic like an inflating balloon, squeezing my lungs against my rib cage.

Mom yanked my door open and said, "Out, Gwen!" through clenched teeth. Then, struggling for a nicer voice, she added, "I'll make lemonade."

But she didn't make lemonade. She collapsed in a heap in front of the TV.

I went to my room and tiptoed in the dark to my window to pull the shade closed. But even so, my skin prickled with the feeling of being watched. I switched on my ceiling light, my reading light, and my radio.

Ricky Ronalds was on. Good, I thought, I could use a laugh. But I listened to a few callers, and their stories were *sad,* not funny. Had they always been sad?

I considered calling in and telling Ricky about *my* messed-up life. But what if someone recognized my voice? I turned off the radio and the room got very, very quiet. There was nothing left to listen to but my thoughts.

My parents had argued in the past, but nothing like now. Now it seemed every word they said to each other was mean and angry. It was all the fault of this awful strike! It was like a disease, I thought, a sickness. My parents had a bad case of the *hate plague!*

Obviously Jess was infected too. I guessed we'd both

caught it. Why else would I have said I rocked the Volkswagen? Why else would she have believed me? It was scary to think we were all hopelessly contaminated—but it made so much sense. I hoped the hate plague wasn't incurable.

What if all wars and fights and divorces were really outbreaks of this same disease? This hate germ, virus, bacteria, whatever. Maybe someone could invent an antibiotic or something and put it in the drinking water. Then everyone would take a sip—and *zing!* Instant peace! Ricky Ronalds would be out of work because there'd be no more unhappy people. At least not *that* kind of unhappy.

We'd all look back and say, "What a shame those zillions of people died in wars and riots and stuff since the beginning of time. Such a waste." But what were the chances of someone finding a cure in time to save *me*?

Mom had a job interview the next morning. She came in to wake me, and held up two outfits on hangers. "It's been a while since I've been on an interview," she said. "Which do you think? The blue pinstripe from the dawn of mankind or the gray silk from the Stone Age?"

"Stone Age," I said, and burrowed back under my covers.

Sometime later Dad pounded on my door. "Hey, lazy, I've got chili cooking."

"For breakfast?" I mumbled. "Yick."

"It's twelve-thirty," he said.

I'd never slept that late before. Not even when I had the flu. I stumbled to the kitchen, where Dad was at the stove. He pointed to the table and said, "Lick those."

"What are they?" I asked.

"Envelopes."

"I can *see* they're envelopes," I said, "but what are they for?"

"Invitations to a costume ball," Dad grumbled.

"Really?"

He rolled his eyes at my stupidity. "Gwen, they're resumes. Job applications."

I flipped the envelopes over and looked at the addresses. All were out of town. Most were out of state. "We're *moving*?" I asked.

Dad shrugged. "We'll see," he said.

I licked the first one. Moving away would mean a fresh start, I thought. It would mean not having to face Jess. But it would also mean no more Gram, Uncle Dave, Aunt Ann, Vicky, my friends at school. It would mean not getting to know Abe. It would mean being The New Kid in a strange place. The last envelope gave me a paper cut on my lip.

Dad put a bowl of chili in front of me. But my tongue felt gummy and tasted like envelope, and the chili smelled—like chili.

The mailman passed by the window. When he dropped our mail into the slot, I waved and called out "Thanks!" as usual.

Dad had disappeared. I thought nothing of it until he came out of the pantry with a strange expression on his face.

"Dad?" I said. "You okay?"

He looked at me and exhaled slowly. Then he said, "Men work. That's what men do. They go to work in the morning and they come home at night. They do *not* stand at the stove stirring chili in the middle of the day."

He didn't say it jokey. He said it straight out. Like hiding from the mailman was reasonable. Like being home was shameful and cooking made it worse. This was so unlike him that I hardly recognized this sexist man as my father.

I shuffled the envelopes, thinking maybe we could find my old dad in a new city. That is, if it wasn't already too late.

I sat on the front steps slapping at mosquitoes and half watching squirrels chase one another across the telephone wire. I was waiting for Vicky and Coach Marty to pick me up on their way to strike headquarters. I wondered what they would say when I told them I was staying with the team. Would they think I was a traitor? Or a spy?

I wondered too why Coach Marty was always the one driving Vicky around, but I figured her mom must have a job. A nonstriking job. I couldn't picture Vicky's mom, but I knew I must've met her. I felt a twinge of shame at realizing that I'd never really paid much attention to any of my teammates—besides Jess, of course.

In the car I said, "I hope the girls who replace the strikers will feel really creepy. They'll be *scab* players!"

"I'd rather you didn't use that word, Gwen," Coach Marty said from the front seat.

"Scab?" I asked, blushing.

"They're just folks trying to get by, like everyone else. Right?"

I was too embarrassed to look up. I'd just been saying what

everyone said. Trying to sound like a striker. And now Coach Marty thought I was bad.

We got to headquarters in time to help drag out tables and chairs. Abe wasn't there.

"They're just starting this soup thing," Vicky explained. "For the people who are seriously broke."

"They're broke already?" I asked, wondering how big a step it was from mowing your own lawn to needing free soup.

Vicky shrugged. "Guess so." She pointed to a woman carrying in a gigantic pot. "That's Mrs. Rhodes. She and her husband are *both* out on strike." Then she nodded toward a mob of kids hunched over coloring books and said, "Those are their kids."

I knew I should tell Vicky that I wasn't leaving the team. But how? I was sure she assumed I was quitting like her and the rest of the strikers' girls. It made me mad at the same time—that I was expected to just fall in place.

"The food's donated," Vicky continued. "Oh, and do you know Mrs. Montez?"

I shook my heavy head.

Vicky poked her chin toward a table where two women were stacking bowls and laughing about something. I didn't know which one Vicky meant, but I figured it didn't matter.

"Her husband's really sick," Vicky whispered.

Neither of them looked like women with sick husbands.

"How do you *know* all this?" I asked.

Vicky giggled. "I eavesdrop!" Then she said, "Everybody's medical insurance stopped as soon as they walked out, you know. So they're taking up a collection to get Mr. Montez to the clinic."

How depressing! I wished Vicky hadn't told me that, and I hoped she wouldn't tell me more. I was searching my brain for a way to change the subject when the two women at the table called, "Come and get it!" They stood, ladles ready to serve.

People lined up, everyone talking and joking. Vicky took a baby out of one woman's arms so the woman could eat. I made myself go up to a lady with twin toddlers and offer to watch them. I was about to tell her that my dad was a twin—but hadn't Dad said *everyone* knew about him and Uncle Dave and that they were watching? I decided maybe it would be better if nobody knew who I was related to.

I led the twins to the tub of raggedy toys. I'd never actually baby-sat, and the only little kid I knew was Riley. But these boys were older than him, so I wasn't sure what to do. I grabbed two stuffed animals and tried to put on a puppet show.

"Once upon a time there were two boys," I said. "One was a teddy bear and one was a bunny, but they were twin brothers, just like you."

"We're snakes!" one twin said.

"We *eat* bunnies!" the other one shrieked. They both cracked up and began hissing and slithering around. So much for my heartwarming tale of brotherly differences.

I pictured my dad and uncle as kids and wondered if one day these happy snakes would act like strangers to each other.

Luckily, they were too busy wiggling to care that I was just sitting like a lump.

After everyone ate and the twins had been fetched by their mom, Vicky pulled me over to a huge metal sink. "Now the fun part," she said, pointing to the enormous stack of dirty bowls.

"We're on KP?" I asked. "Yick!"

Vicky laughed and handed me my first bowl. "Dinner dishes at home will be a breeze after this!" she said as cheerfully as ever.

"You smile too much," I said, only half kidding.

Vicky made an exaggerated frown. "Better?" she asked.

"Well, doesn't any of this bum you out?" I asked. "Don't you think it's depressing or scary at all?"

Vicky thought for a second, then said, "Some of the stories around here are sad. And I know I'll miss playing ball. And yeah, I guess it's a little scary, but mostly it's interesting. Mostly it's *not* boring."

"I like boring," I said. And Vicky, of course, laughed, which made me blurt out, "How come you're so nice to me all the time? I know I'm a drag to be with."

Vicky looked down and scrubbed the bowl in her hands. She seemed embarrassed.

"Sorry," I mumbled. "Forget I said that."

"No, no. That's okay," Vicky said, still concentrating on the bowl. "You don't remember, do you?"

"Remember what?" I asked.

"Last year? When I joined the team to replace Deanne after her car accident? And the others were picking on me as if *I'd* been the one who broke Deanne's leg?"

"Huh?"

"You came up and acted so friendly to me—to show that *you* didn't blame me for the car accident or whatever. And then everyone else chilled out and acted normal. Remember?"

I didn't.

"That was brave of you," Vicky said. "And I'll never forget it. If you hadn't come to my rescue, who knows how horrendous last summer would've been for me?"

It was my turn to be embarrassed. Vicky thought I'd been heroic, but probably I'd had no idea that she was being picked on back then. Maybe I'd been *accidentally* nice to her, which didn't mean squat. It certainly didn't make me anything special.

Why was I always getting credit and blame for things I didn't do on purpose? Things that were just accidents. Didn't I have any say over my own life?

The answer was clearly *No*. My life had nothing to do with me—it just *happened* to me. I was like a scrap of litter being flown around by a leaf blower. I felt a shudder move all the way through me, and that's when I knew I was off the team.

Maybe I'd always known, I thought—from the second I saw Dad at the kitchen table in the middle of a work day. Or from the moment they told me Jess wasn't coming to the picket line.

When didn't matter, I told myself. All that mattered was

that I knew now. I'd been stupid to think I could fight it. Stupid to think I could make my own decision. Stupid to think it was up to me—that I could ignore the strike, show up for practice, play ball, act normal, and get away with it. It had always been hopeless.

My world had gone insane and I had to go with it.

Chapter Eight
THE GRAND SLAM PLAN

MY HANDS WERE washing the bowls, but my mind was drenched in self-pity until I heard: "Well, if it ain't the union maids!" I turned around and there was Abe, tossing a ball from hand to hand. "Anyone wanna play?" he asked. "Or do you have to mop the floors next?" The two boys with him laughed. One had a bat.

I flicked soapsuds at Abe and said, "You're on!"

When we got outside, the boy named Jose said, "Don't worry, we'll go easy on you ladies."

"No need for that!" Vicky said. And I agreed: "Give us all you've got." But they lobbed us slow, wimpy pitches as if we were made of glass.

When I slammed Abe's pitch over the fence, he said, "Not bad, for a *girl*. A little more practice and you might make a halfway decent player—considering."

I didn't appreciate that crack. Then the other boys, Zack and Jose, made a bunch of antigirl comments too. Maybe their teasing wouldn't have bugged me if life had been normal, but under the circumstances I had no patience to spare. Plus I couldn't believe the boys thought more meanness was funny— as if there weren't enough bad feelings in the air already.

The last straw was when Zack suggested Vicky and I get six strikes instead of three. That's when I launched the ball into the stratosphere and threw down the bat. "I've had it," I said, and huffed off the field—with Vicky right behind me.

"What's wrong?" Abe asked, as if he didn't know.

"Okay, *eight* strikes, then! How's that?" Zack called after us.

"And we'll catch left-handed!" Jose added.

Vicky and I ignored them and stomped inside to play Ping-Pong.

"Those smug, self-important, supreme *idiots*," Vicky said. "They're as bad as the boys at my school."

"Mine too," I said. "I'd sure love to teach them a lesson." And that's when I got my idea.

I was dying to tell Vicky, but there were people everywhere. I grabbed the Ping-Pong paddle out of her hand and pulled her toward the door.

"Not back outside!" she protested. "I *just* stopped sweating." But I hurried her out behind the building, away from where the boys were playing. Luckily, there was a triangle of shade on the back steps.

I sat her down there and said, "I have a softball idea."

"Yeah," she said. "My dad thinks we could still get on the County League."

"No, no. I don't mean a league." I lowered my voice. "I'm thinking of *one* game. A game between two teams that have been at war since . . . do you want a hint?"

Vicky nodded.

"Since Adam and Eve!"

"Us against the boys!" she shrieked. "Yes!"

I shushed her, then whispered, "Here's how I figure it: We'll tell all the girls that the boys have challenged us to a game. I know it's a tiny lie, but it'll be worth it. Jess and I aren't great pals right now, but I bet she'd round up the management girls. You and I'll get the strikers. Strike or no, I'm positive that every single girl is just *dying* to beat the boys' team!"

"Absolutely!" Vicky squealed. Then, catching herself, she clamped her hand over her mouth and giggled.

"Then we challenge the boys," I whispered. "There's no way Abe and his friends could walk away from *that*! They know we'd laugh them out of town if they couldn't get their team together to face us."

"You're a genius! An absolute *genius*!" Vicky hooted, giving me squeeze.

I started imagining the scene: Before the boys' team shows up, two stiff armies of girls approach the ball field/battlefield. General Jess leads the management troops. I lead the strikers. It's up to us to make peace within our ranks—quick—before the boys come!

I raise my imaginary phone. "Hello?" I say.

Jess is holding hers. "Hello. Who's this?" she asks with the tiniest hint of a smile.

But just as I was thinking of what I'd say to make all the girls reunite as a team, Vicky interrupted my thoughts.

"It'll be a grand slam!" she said. "First, it'll get our team back together." She held up her thumb. "Second, we'll cream the boys and shut them up once and for all." She wiggled her index finger. "And third, the negotiators'll look down from their windows, see all us kids playing ball, and realize what turds they're being. They'll immediately end the strike—just in time to watch us kick the boys' butts!"

I giggled. "Maybe we should let it be a tie. So everyone's totally happy."

"I can live with that," Vicky agreed. "As long as we trounce them later, in a play-off."

We both cracked up.

Then I said, "But that's only three RBIs! Unite our team, trounce the boys, end the strike—what's the fourth?"

"Be heroes!" Vicky exclaimed. "We'll be famous! They'll name streets after us! Sing songs about us!"

"They'll have a parade in our honor!" I squealed. "Marching bands, baton twirlers, the works! We'll ride on a huge float—waving to our fans!" Vicky and I giggled and waved like beauty queens to the imaginary crowd surrounding the steps. "It sounds like a movie!" I said.

Vicky nodded, grinning eagerly. "It *does*!"

"It sounds *too* much like a movie," I realized out loud.

Vicky's smile sank a little and I felt like a fool. If Jess had been there, she'd have made a crack about my "big ideas."

"Stuff like that doesn't happen in real life," I sighed, defeated. "They *have* a team of girls. *Press Gazette* girls can play *Press Gazette* boys any time they want. They don't need us." The steps suddenly felt hard and uncomfortable. The heat was unbearable.

Vicky plucked the weed growing next to her and twirled it in her hand. "It was a great idea," she said. "But you know, Marsha's parents shipped her off to camp the second they pulled her from the team. I got a postcard from her."

"I didn't know you were friends," I said.

"Me and Marsha? Not like you and Jess or anything, but we're friends, sure. And Liza's dad got a job in Indiana or Idaho. Some *I* state. They moved last weekend."

I hadn't known *that* either. It felt weird that the other girls were keeping in touch. Did they think I was a snob, or mean or something? Had they hated Jess and me all along for only hanging around with each other? If so, they never let it show.

Vicky was saying, "Illinois, Iowa. Did you ever notice how many states start with *I*?"

"Was Liza glad to go?" I asked, remembering Dad's envelopes.

Vicky shrugged. "Mixed. You heard about that scene in the market, right? When Liza and her mom ran into Trina's mom?"

"No. What scene?" I asked, although I suspected I didn't really want to know.

"Well, Trina's mom looked at Liza's mom's groceries and

complained that Liza's family could sit on their lazy, worthless buns and eat *steak*—while wonderful, decent, working folk like herself could only afford pork snouts."

"She *said* that?" I gasped.

"Well, maybe not 'pork snouts,'" Vicky said, giggling, "but you know what I mean."

I opened my mouth but Vicky added, "There's more! Liza's mom got so mad, she smashed a dozen super-jumbo eggs in Mrs. Johnson's shopping cart!"

"No way!"

Vicky nodded. "I swear! Eggs everywhere!"

"Then what happened?"

"Well, then I guess Mrs. Johnson went nuts too and threatened to sue. And the store manager got into it. He told them to leave—without their food. Liza said it was pretty embarrassing, really. Getting thrown out. People staring at them. Having her mom treated like a lunatic."

"Yick!" I said, suddenly feeling creeped out.

We were both quiet a minute. Then Vicky said, "So, even if the strike settled today and my dad got hired back as coach, it *still* wouldn't be the old team, not without Liza and Marsha."

"I'd been hoping we'd somehow finish out the season," I confessed with my last ounce of energy. "Maybe still end up champs."

Vicky laughed. "I'd watch *that* movie."

I closed my eyes to keep the tears inside my head and the world out.

• • •

When I got home, I went straight to my room and took my team pictures off the wall—one by one. I tried not to look at Jess, smiling her photo-smile. But I couldn't help glancing at the earliest shot—of the two of us still practically babies, posing so proudly in our miniature uniforms.

I shoved the pictures in my closet and crammed my trophies and uniform in there too. Then I lay down on my bed, feeling so heavy that my back seemed to press clear through the mattress.

I looked at my blank wall. There were rectangles where the pictures had hung. Rectangular ghosts—left to haunt me. I shut my eyes, but the rectangles still dangled in my mind.

I hauled myself up out of the bed and went looking for Dad, to ask if I could paint my room.

Just then, Mom came in the front door and called out, "Yoo-hoo!" She dropped her portfolio on the table and announced, "They liked me!"

"Everyone likes you," Dad said, coming in from the kitchen, but something was sour in his voice. Mom either didn't hear or chose to ignore his tone.

"Well, they *really* liked me," she said. "They asked if I'd start Monday, and I said yes!"

"Congratulations," Dad said with a stiff smile and no enthusiasm.

"Monday?" I asked. "*This* Monday?"

Mom smiled. "Wait till they see that I only have two outfits." She giggled. "My first paycheck goes for work clothes."

I still couldn't quite get it. "A real leave-in-the-morning, come-home-at-night, five-days-a-week kind of job?"

Mom nodded. She seemed happy, and that was good. But I'd always thought she *liked* working at home, being here with me. I guess I was just plain wrong about *everything* these days.

My brain flashed a memory of cold winter days after school, Mom and me sharing the living room couch—our heads propped at either end and our tangled legs cozy under the woolly afghan. Sometimes we'd have a fire in the fireplace and a pot of apple cinnamon tea on the coffee table.

Mom took off her shoes and rubbed her feet. "It's a small ad agency," she said. "Seem like friendly people. Not a bad commute. It's just up near the mall."

"Do they buy advertising space in the scab paper?" Dad asked.

Mom's smile fell. "Oh," she said. "I forgot to ask."

Dad didn't even try to keep the smile in place. "You *forgot?*" His voice dripped with scorn. "Well, maybe you ought to call them back and find out."

I didn't want to hear more. I beat it out of there and went back to my room. The expression "broken home" occurred to me. My home was breaking. I could hear the walls cracking. I could feel them crumbling.

Paint wouldn't help.

My game schedule was taped to the back of my door. I was about to rip it up, but first I looked at it. We—no, *they* had a home game tomorrow against Water and Power. I wondered how weird it was for Jess playing there without me.

What if it had been Jess who'd had to leave the team? Would I have played without her?

Then I realized that I didn't know for sure that Jess was

staying on the team. Mad as she was at me for my lie about the Volkswagen, she must've known it was a lie. And maybe she decided that staying on the team without me, and without Vicky and Marsha and Liza and Coach Marty, wasn't right.

As if on cue, Mom called out, "Gwen, Jess's on the phone." My heart leapt. I knew, as I ran for the phone, that Jess was calling to make everything better!

I grabbed the phone and gasped a breathless "Hello?"

"I can't believe you did that!" Jess snarled. "I just *cannot* believe you skipped practice!"

"Huh? There was a practice today?"

"Don't play dumb!"

"No one told me," I said.

"Yeah, right," Jess scoffed.

"It's *true*! No one called!"

"You're just a quitter. A chicken. You didn't even *tell* anyone you weren't coming. Coach Alex didn't have a *clue!*"

"Coach who?" I asked.

"He told *me* to call you—like *I'm* responsible for you!" Jess practically spat. "Do you have any idea how embarrassing it was when everyone asked me where you were?"

I couldn't speak.

"Just like your dad and all the strikers!" Jess said. "Things get a little uncomfortable—you're not getting your way—so do you stay and work it out? No. You just turn and run."

Ouch! Her voice burned with such hot *hate* that I slammed down the receiver automatically, like pulling my hand from a flame. Then I stared at the phone, half expecting it to lash out and singe me again.

Jess hated me.

I knew she could be mad at me; we'd been getting mad at each other since birth. But *hate* was new.

I looked up. Both my parents were standing in the doorway. I closed my eyes. There was nowhere to hide but behind my own eyelids, and it wasn't even safe there. My mind was a mass of injuries—pain everywhere my thoughts touched.

"Did you know about a practice today?" I asked from behind closed lids. "Did anyone call?"

They said no.

I knew I'd be able to tell if they were lying, if I opened my eyes and looked at them. But I kept my eyes shut. What did it really matter if Coach Alex—whoever he was—didn't call me or I didn't call him? Either way, I was off the team. I'd known that already, but I guess there's a difference between knowing and *knowing*.

Back in my room I felt my face twist, but no tears came out, only strangled gags that left me choking.

Chapter Nine
CIVIL WAR

"WAKE UP THIS INSTANT!" boomed the voice of my grandmother, making me jump. There she was, hands on her hips, looming like a totem pole at the foot of my bed.

"Hi, Gram," I said.

"Don't you Hi-Gram *me,* miss! You get up and dressed this instant!" She snatched yesterday's clothes off the floor and threw them on the bed, scolding, "What foolishness! Like some Victorian sissy in a swoon, for heaven's sake." Then she shook her finger at me and said, "I will not tolerate ninnies in this family! Do you hear me?"

I heard her.

"I'm going to my car," she said. "You better be dressed and

out there in four minutes, tops!" Then she marched down the hall, muttering, "I've never seen such nonsense. Perfectly healthy child acting like some delicate, lily-livered . . ." I looked at the clock; it was eleven-fifteen. I dressed quickly.

Dad nodded to me as I passed him on my way out the door. As soon as I got my seat belt snapped, Gram pulled away from the curb and headed for the waterfront. We were both silent during the drive. Gram parked next to the wharf, then turned to me and demanded, "What's going on between you and Jess?"

My head snapped around. "She *told* you?"

"No, she did not," Gram said. "But you came down separately for dinner and sat on opposite sides of my table." Gram raised her eyebrows at me. "And I didn't hear giggles."

A river barge slid into view. "You knew something was wrong because we didn't sit together and giggle?" I asked. "Even though there was all that other stuff going on?"

"Precisely," she said. "Now talk."

So I talked—about everything. About Jess taking Nay-ah's side, about my telling her that Dad and I rocked the Volkswagen. About my being made to quit the team and no one even telling me there was a practice. "Here's what I think. I think this strike is bigger than we are," I said at the end. "I think it's too hard for Jess and me to be friends."

Gram grunted. "Nonsense."

I shrugged. "Well, she's proud that her dad can put out his newspaper without *my* dad. And where does that leave me?"

"How important was the newspaper to your friendship before the strike?" Gram asked.

"It wasn't."

"Well then," Gram said, as if something had been settled. But I was more confused than ever.

Gram started the car and backed away from the wharf. When we joined the traffic, I asked where we were going.

"Where do you think?"

"Jess's house?" I asked, hoping I was wrong—and hoping I was right.

Gram nodded.

At Jess's she told me to wait in the car. I watched her march up to the door and knock her one loud knock. Then she disappeared inside. I waited, feeling happier each minute. I knew Gram would fix everything. She always did.

I remembered Mom joking, back when she still joked, that if it dared to rain on our family picnic, the clouds better look out! Gram would be after them with worse than thunderbolts and lightning!

But Gram reappeared alone. First I thought Jess had refused to see me, but then I remembered she had a game today.

"She's not home," Gram said.

"I know."

"She's at a game."

"I figured that."

Then I realized Gram didn't know what to do next. I'd never imagined a situation that could stump Gram. But first there'd been the dinner at her condo, when the dads wouldn't talk, and now this. I didn't like it.

"We could pick her up from the game," I suggested.

Gram nodded (one nod) and told me to run in and tell

Aunt Ann that we'd pick up Jess. So I did. But once I was back in Gram's car and we were on our way, I wondered if I was ready to actually see Jess in uniform.

"Pull over!" I cried. "I've changed my mind."

"Better to face things head-on," Gram said, her resolve restored. "It'll be fine."

I hoped she was right. I nervously scratched mosquito bites till my legs were streaked with blood.

When we reached the field, I said, "How 'bout if I wait here and you nab her when the game's over?"

Gram said, "Okay." She opened the windows, cut the engine, then hauled herself out of the car and stalked toward the stands.

With the air-conditioning gone, it was murderously hot in no time. Sweat dribbled down my back, and my hair stuck to my face. I watched the heat squiggle over the car's hood. It was unbearable. Gram's car was so tidy that there wasn't anything lying around to fan myself with. I got out and leaned against the bumper, but there was no breeze, so I moved into the shadow of the building nearby.

Then I couldn't resist sneaking closer, still in the shade, until I could see Jess on the pitcher's mound. She was winding up, concentrating, thinking about the game. Certainly not thinking about me.

I was so jealous, I could taste it. I suddenly missed playing ball more than I ever thought possible. I missed the feel of the bat, the sound of the ball landing in my glove. I missed working as a team. Even the fear of striking out or muffing a play—even *losing*—seemed heavenly compared to not playing at all. Everything about it seemed impossibly wonderful and far away.

Why was I the one being punished? Why was Jess the one playing ball? Was it fair that my family was going broke while hers wasn't? How about the fact that my parents could barely stand each other—was *that* fair?

I ran back to the car and threw myself down on the scorching-hot seat. As the sweat poured out of me, I found myself whimpering, "It's just not fair. It's just not fair."

I heard a big cheer and knew the game was over. It wouldn't be long now. I peeled my thighs off the seat and tried to pull myself together.

Girls started leaving. The first one from my team was Trina. She was with her mom. Uh-oh! Mrs. Johnson spotted me and marched up to the car. "What are you doing here?" she asked, sticking her big head in the window.

"Nothing," I squeaked.

She narrowed her eyes. "We don't want any trouble," she said.

"Me neither."

Trina tugged her mother's arm. "Momma!" she cried. "Come on!"

Mrs. Johnson peered harder at me, drilling a warning into my skull. "You people got no business here," she said.

I nodded, then shook my head, trying to look agreeable and harmless.

Finally, she stomped away with Trina in tow.

I melted low in my seat. What kind of trouble did she

think I'd cause? Did she think I was armed? Did she think I'd lob grenades onto the ball field?

She turned back to nail me with one last threatening look.

I scrunched my eyes shut and didn't open them again until I heard the car doors open. Gram grunted, getting behind the wheel, and Jess slid into the backseat. I turned around and said, "Hi."

"Hi," Jess said. No smile.

Gram rolled up the windows and blasted the air-conditioning. She drove to her condo and hurried us inside. No one had said anything since those two small hi's.

Gram pointed to the stairs leading up to her loft and said, "Don't come down until this is resolved." Then she handed Jess a little silver bell and added, "If negotiations go long, you may ring for refreshments."

I climbed the stairs behind Jess, thinking that this was exactly what Gram wanted to do to our dads—send them to their room until they'd fixed everything and come out pals. I smiled. Mom was right: If Gram was at the bargaining table, the strike would've ended long ago.

Jess sat stiffly on the edge of Gram's bed. I pretended to shy away from Lamp Ghost—kidding, making a little *joke*. But Jess just blinked slowly, as if I were thoroughly annoying.

So I put my hand up in our phone salute. "Hello?"

Jess still didn't smile. She lifted her invisible receiver reluctantly, as if it weighed a ton. "Who's this?" she asked in a weary voice.

"It's m-me," I stammered. "I just wanted you to know that

Dad and I didn't really touch Linea's mom's car. We were nowhere near it."

Jess looked blankly at me, as if I'd spoken gibberish. No, as if I hadn't spoken at all.

I kept talking. "I just said it because I was so mad at you that for a second I'd sort of wished I *had* given that car a shove or two." I smiled a bit but Jess didn't. "Anyway," I said, "I'm sorry."

I don't know what I'd expected, but all Jess did was shrug and say, "Okay," in an empty voice.

"Okay?" It didn't *feel* okay.

"Okay, I get it," she said, standing. She didn't hang up her phone, but I hung up mine anyway, feeling stupid.

It would have been a good time for her to say something about how sorry she was that she was still on the team. Or that she was sorry about *something*. But she didn't. She just turned toward the stairs.

"Jess, wait," I said.

She shifted from one foot to the other, not quite looking at me. I'd already confessed my lie. I'd admitted to being a jerk. What more did she want me to say?

"I really didn't know about that practice," I said. "Coach Whatever-his-name-is never called me. I swear."

"Well, he says he did."

I shook my head.

Jess's voice was cold as death. "Do you honestly expect me to believe that he called every girl but you?"

"Yes."

"Why would I believe that?"

"Because it's true."

"So says the girl who spit on—or *didn't* spit on—Linea's mom's car. It gets hard to keep track."

"Spit? Gross! It was rocked and hit, not spit on. No one spit."

Jess gave me a withering look, as if I were dreary scum. then she went downstairs.

I'd learned that in civil wars families were torn apart. This felt like that. It didn't matter how close we used to be; now that we'd come apart so far, the past no longer meant a thing.

I followed Jess down. I knew Gram was going to be disappointed. She closed her book and looked from me to Jess. Then she slowly shook her head and said, "What is this family coming to?"

In the car on the way home, Gram clutched the steering wheel and concentrated on her driving as if she were navigating through fog. I noticed for the first time that she was old.

There must be a single moment, I thought, when whole countries go from trying to work out their problems to being so mad that they don't want to talk about it anymore. Forget peace. They just want to declare war—get out guns and bombs and blow one another to smithereens. I could tell Jess was feeling that way about me now.

But *she's* the one wearing the uniform, I fumed. She's the one playing softball as always. And *she* won't accept *my* apology?

My mishmash of feelings finally came together in one solid clump of anger. What right did Jess have to stonewall me? How dare she? She should be begging my forgiveness.

I didn't actually want to *kill* her, but I hoped I'd never have to see her again—ever.

Chapter Ten
A SUMMER WITHOUT SOFTBALL

I WAS STILL in bed when Mom came to say good-bye Monday morning. She seemed as excited and nervous about her first day on the job as I used to get before games.

The house felt instantly empty, even though Dad was home. It wasn't as if Mom never left the house before, but this was different.

I stared at my ceiling, trying to think of a reason to get up. What would I do today? I would've asked Dad to play catch with me, but there was no reason to practice. And he was never in a ball-playing kind of mood anymore.

How was I supposed to fill a whole *summer* without softball if I couldn't even think of a way to fill one morning?

There were board games in my closet and a deck of cards in my desk. There was the TV in the den. But those things were for winter days when there was nothing outside but frostbite. Summer was for swinging the bat, running to base, catching the ball.

I supposed I could ask Dad to drive me to the pool. I tried to picture myself acting casual, pretending to be happy swimming alone, standing in line for a snack alone, *being* alone. Not possible.

I sat up. I thought about calling Vicky, but I was afraid she would think I was just using her now that Jess hated me.

It was hot and sticky, and I wanted to run through the sprinklers at least, but that too seemed pathetic to do alone. So I lay back down to mope and sweat.

"Phone!" Dad called.

I got up too fast and felt dizzy, but I ran. It was Vicky inviting me over. I was so grateful, I almost cried. Dad grumbled about the distance, but finally agreed to drop me off on his way to the picket line.

I guess I'd expected Vicky's house to be more or less like all the other houses I'd ever been to, but it wasn't. It was an itty-bitty dollhouse of a trailer with a postage stamp–sized yard, surrounded by lots of other trailers with tiny yards. I loved it instantly.

Coach Marty's feet were sticking out from under his car. Dad bent over to talk engines with him while Vicky pulled me into her living room. There was a birdcage in the corner.

"Meet Tweet," Vicky said, smiling at a little yellow bird. I remembered her saying that ever since the strike, she'd been lining her bird's cage with toilet paper, and it was true!

Vicky gave me the full tour, which took about four seconds. I saw her bedroom with its curtains the size of napkins. Then she showed me Coach Marty's room, crammed with baseball trophies.

Vicky said, "This is my dad's room," not "This is my parents' room." I wondered what happened to her mom, but I didn't ask.

Then we went to the kitchen and she pulled a pitcher of fruit punch out of her mini-refrigerator.

"I saw our *ex*-team yesterday," I told her. "But just for a split second."

"They played Water and Power, right?" Vicky said. "Who won?"

I shrugged. I hadn't asked. I suppose I should have.

"Did you meet the six replacements?" Vicky asked.

"Six?"

"You, me, Liza, Marsha." Vicky ticked them off on her fingers. "Plus the two management girls, Annabel and Linea."

"*Linea?* Linea quit the team?" This was news to me. I'd assumed Jess and Linea were spending all their time together—like Vicky and me.

"She left town a couple days after the Volkswagen thing. Didn't you know that?"

I shook my head just as Coach Marty banged through the tiny screen door, calling, "Next stop: headquarters!" We chugged our drinks and followed him out to the car.

"Six?" I said in the car. "That's half the team!"

Vicky laughed. "It took you that long to do the math?"

I'm no math whiz, but what really took so long was trying to picture the team with so many new players, and imagining Jess there without Nay-ah.

Ha! I thought, in a mustache-twirling way. Serves Jess right! But the hee-hee turned first into a sinking guilt, as if her loneliness were my fault—and last, into pity. I couldn't imagine how I would've gotten through the past weeks without Vicky. All alone? All the time? The thought gave me shivers.

But I didn't want to feel bad for Jess, so I shook my head, clearing out all thoughts of her.

I leaned toward the front seat. "Who's this Alex guy?" I asked Coach Marty.

"The new coach? He's a sportswriter," Coach Marty said. "Nice chap."

I sat back to let my mind chew on *that!* How could he be "nice" and take Coach Marty's place? He *had* to be management. Well, Uncle Dave's management, and *he's* nice. I felt myself getting sleepy. I fought it by opening my eyes wide.

"Being awake makes me so tired," I told Vicky.

She laughed, of course, thinking it was a joke. Vicky could find humor in anything.

Abe and his friends were playing catch in front of the building. Vicky pulled two gloves out of Coach Marty's trunk and tossed me one. Then she faced the boys and yelled, "Any of your stupid sexist cracks and we're out of here!"

Abe mimed zipping his lips shut. Then he threw me a fast-ball—and a huge smile. If he thought that smile would make me miss the ball, he was wrong. It landed square in my glove and I smirked right back at him.

I'd never been a fabulous fielder; hitting was my strength. But lately I'd been catching everything that came my way—even when thrown by Abe. I bet this would've been my best season ever.

When we took a soda break, I noticed that Zack was drinking very carefully around a swollen lip. It looked like the huge spider bite I'd gotten on my chin once.

"What happened to you?" I asked him.

"Me? Nothin'." Zack grinned. "But you shoulda seen the other guy." Then he winked at Jose and Abe, who started poking each other and winking back.

"What other guy?" I asked.

"We went to the game last night," Abe snickered. "Saw some old friends." This made them fall all over laughing.

"You got in a fight?" Vicky asked. "With guys from your team?"

"I didn't say that!" Abe answered, getting fake-innocent and wide-eyed. "Did *you* say that?"

"Not me!" Jose said, thumping himself on the chest. "I didn't say nothin'!"

And Zack said, "I just bumped into a wall. Right, guys?"

Abe and Jose laughed their stupid heads off, saying, "Sure thing!" "Absolutely!" "A wall!" "Old Zack here bumped into a wall!"

Vicky and I marched off in disgust. I couldn't believe I'd almost thought Abe might be a halfway decent guy. Yick!

• • •

At around six Vicky and Coach Marty dropped me off at home. "See ya later, Vicky," I said as I got out of the car. "Thanks for the ride, Coach Marty."

"You're very welcome," he said. "But, Gwen, from now on you can just call me Marty or Your Excellency. Or Hey You."

I got it, but I couldn't imagine it. "Yes, sir," I said.

He laughed. "*Sir* is good. I can get behind *Sir!*"

Mom pulled up just as Coach Marty and Vicky drove away. We trudged to the front door together, Mom dragging.

"That man doesn't want me calling him Coach anymore," I told her, trying to joke instead of choke.

"Makes sense," she said, kicking off her shoes, then peeling off her panty hose.

Dad came out of the kitchen, wiped his hands on a towel, and grumbled that dinner was nearly ready. Before all this, Dad had never done much in the kitchen. He didn't look thrilled with it now, and I remembered him hiding from the mailman.

Mom sank into a chair and grunted in response.

"How was your first day?" I asked.

She sighed.

At dinner Dad asked if I'd like to go to Gram's while he was picketing the next day. "When I called there today, she barely spoke to me," he said. "Must still be miffed that Dave and I didn't end the strike as per her orders."

I guessed that meant Gram hadn't told him about my botched meeting with Jess.

"Your mother is used to being obeyed," Mom said. "It's

inconceivable to her that *anything* could be more than she and her big, tough sons could handle."

Hey! I'd thought Mom was *proud* that Gram was so strong, but now she sounded sarcastic about it. I thought Mom loved Gram. Was I wrong about that too?

After dinner I curled up on my bed. I heard Dad leave for another meeting or the picket line or whatever. Mom had the TV on. She'd never watched so much television before. And I'd never been so tired in my life. Hate Plague symptoms, I thought.

Then suddenly it was morning, and Dad was in my room saying, "Gwen, this Sleeping Beauty act is getting a little old."

I rubbed my eyes and stretched. Dad yanked open my curtains. "I'm sorry you've been caught in the strike," he said, not sounding very sorry, "but these are grown-up problems and you shouldn't let them upset you."

I'd have to be totally numb not to let them affect me, I thought. Numb or dead. Adults make *their* problems *everyone's* problems.

"Now get up on your hind legs," he said, "and get dressed. Mom's left for work, and I need to hurry to a meeting. You'll have to come with me, unless you want me to drop you at Jess's or something."

Jess's? Had Dad really not noticed that Jess and I were never together anymore?

I didn't want to hang around some boring meeting with my dad, so I searched my sleepy brain for someone I could call—some friend from school who hadn't gone to camp or on a family vacation. Someone who had nothing to do with the strike.

I couldn't think of a soul, so I called Vicky. As the phone rang, I wondered again how Jess was filling her non-softball time without me and without Linea. But Jess brought this on herself by dumping me like that, I told myself. It was her decision, not mine.

I wasn't even sure *why* she was so angry. Because she thought I'd really rocked the Volkswagen? Or because I lied about it? And what was that about spitting? How gross!

I had half forgotten I'd dialed the phone until Vicky answered, sounding breathless. She'd heard it from outside. She said they were just leaving for strike headquarters and that I should meet her there.

I was sick of headquarters. I didn't know how Vicky could stand being so *helpful* all the time. The babies, the soup, the whole scene—people pretending to be happy when their lives were a mess. People needing to take up collections for one another. It was all so *depressing*! But there was nowhere else for me to go.

Abe's bike wasn't in the bike rack outside headquarters. Good, I thought. He was a jerk—getting into a fistfight like some kind of lint-for-brains macho thug.

I found Vicky inside, trying to teach a song with hand movements to a squirming bunch of little kids. She had a terrible singing voice that almost made me smile. The kids were way more interested in poking one another and giggling than in listening to Vicky.

Finally she threw her arms up in the air, crossed her eyes, and said, "I give up!"

The kids tore off to play, and Vicky and I went to the Ping-Pong table. She told me that some striking drivers got arrested the night before and thrown in jail. They'd been caught smashing the windshields of the newspaper delivery trucks so no one else could drive them.

"That's disgusting!" I said.

"And guess what they used! *Baseball bats!*" Vicky said, as if that was the worst part of the crime. Then she told me that Abe's dad was a driver.

Father—son. Fistfights—vandalism. Same—same, I thought. It serves him right! But then another part of my brain thought, Ouch! Poor Abe.

"Was Abe's dad arrested?" I asked. But Vicky didn't know.

Then she said she'd seen Corey and Joy, two management girls from our ex-team, at the mall last night, but when Coach Marty waved to them, they pretended not to see him. And when he turned his back, they stuck their tongues out at Vicky!

"What did you do?" I asked, half hoping it was something awful, and half afraid it would turn out that Vicky was just as bad as Abe and his dad and the rest of them.

"Nothing," she confessed. "But ask me what I *wish* I'd done!"

I giggled, mostly with relief. I wondered what I would've done. Punched them in the nose? Melted into a puddle? I didn't want to find out. I vowed to myself to avoid all the places where I might run into *anyone*—even if it meant staying home for the rest of my life.

We played Ping-Pong, carried babies around while their moms ate soup, washed bowls, and played Hearts. It was a long day. Abe never did show up. Was he visiting his father in jail?

When Dad came to get me, I watched him pat people on the back and joke around. I remembered that jokey dad. Wow! Had it only been a few weeks since he'd been Grim, Evil Monster of the Deep? It felt like years.

Then a man picked up a megaphone and announced, "Workers, listen up! The *Press Gazette* fireworks have been canceled!"

My insides twisted. But everyone else cheered. Why were they *happy*? I thought everyone *loved* fireworks. Then the man held up his hand for quiet and bellowed, "Our strike is the first thing to stop the fireworks since World War Two!"

More cheering. Wild, out-of-control cheering. I didn't dare look up at my dad. I couldn't bear it if he was cheering too. I ducked out of the building and dashed to the car. It was locked, so I stooped down and cowered in its shadow until Dad came out.

Neither of us said anything in the car. I guessed that the mayor, or whoever was in charge of these things, canceled the fireworks, figuring that strikers and management couldn't be in the same place without a riot breaking out.

I wouldn't have been allowed up to the penthouse this year anyway, I realized—unless there was a last-minute truce. Hey! Maybe that was the point of canceling the fireworks! Maybe it was a bluff to trick the negotiators into a quick settlement. It could work. Just in the nick of time they'd say, "Olly, Olly, all in free! Strike's over!" Then everyone would *really* cheer! The fireworks would be a gigantic celebration!

I smiled at Dad, but from the look on his face I knew he was thinking realistic thoughts, not *movie* thoughts. I sighed, and felt hope fall from me like a tiny raft down a waterfall.

Chapter Eleven
A FINALE WITH HICCUPS

I WAS TRYING to help Dad make dinner, but he didn't like the way I cut green beans. "At an angle!" he barked, as if it mattered. "*Always* cut green beans at an *angle!*"

"Since when do you care?" I asked.

"Since I was demoted to housewife," he answered, practically snarling.

To change the subject I asked him if Abe's father was one of the drivers who got arrested.

"How'd you hear about that?" he asked me back.

"Vicky told me."

"Marty tells that kid too much," he grumbled, making me

wonder what *else* I didn't know about the strike violence. The red Volkswagen rocked in my mind.

Mom came home and we sat down to a very, very quiet dinner. "Pass the green beans" was about as friendly as it got.

After the dishes Mom went into the living room and turned on the television. I went too, but the sound of happy actors laughing in our gloomy house was too creepy. Was Mom just watching so she wouldn't have to talk to me? Maybe she had the volume so loud to kill any chance of conversation.

"Did you hear they canceled the fireworks?" I tried.

Mom nodded without taking her eyes off the screen.

"Don't you think that's going a little far?" I asked her profile.

"Gwen, please," she said in her leave-me-alone voice.

Dad wandered into the room.

"This is the worst summer of my life!" I blurted. "Everything about it stinks! No softball. No fun. I'm bored to death!"

"Bored?" Dad scoffed. "You're *bored*?"

"Well, couldn't we take a trip or something?" I asked. "All this is so dull and—"

"That has to be the most selfish thing I've ever heard!" Dad yelled. "Forget our dwindling savings. Forget the total insecurity of our existence. Bring in the clowns! Let's take a *trip*! Miss All-I-Care-About-Is-Myself is *bored!* Have you given a moment's thought to anyone else? To the lives being destroyed all around you?"

I couldn't see through my tears, but I heard Mom snap at Dad, "Bill, don't dump your troubles on her! A *depressed* little girl."

"And I suppose that's my fault too?" Dad barked, and stormed out of the room.

My mother looked at me. "Don't worry about it, Gwen," she sighed. "Go play." Then she turned back to her television show.

Go play? The "depressed little girl" should go *play*?

My life is a complete mess, I thought. My parents hate each other and they aren't too crazy about me either. My cousin hates me too, and the only friend I have left is Vicky, and she's *insanely* cheerful all the time, although she has nothing to be cheerful about.

And now my parents are probably going to get divorced just like hers. Mom has her new job here; Dad's looking for jobs in other states. I'll end up living with just one of them, like Vicky does—that is, if either of them even *wants* me.

Of course I'm depressed! I thought. Who wouldn't be? I trudged back to my room.

Did Vicky's parents' marriage fall apart the same way? I wondered. Maybe Coach Marty and Vicky's mom were just having a normal fight until the Hate Plague took over, forcing one of them to make mean phone calls or dump paint on the other one's car or something—and after that, there was no turning back.

Would there be any turning back for my parents? Could they still kiss and make up after all these squabbles?

I wondered again about Vicky's mom. Vicky had never said a word about her and I'd never asked. Maybe I should have. Maybe Vicky wanted to talk about her but thought I didn't care. Maybe I just didn't seem like the kind of person you talk to about stuff like that.

Vicky never complained. I could easily picture her as one of those brave girls in war stories, sneaking food to people in hiding. Or carrying messages for the Resistance. She could be an army nurse on the front line, comforting dying soldiers while bullets whiz by. Vicky—washing soup bowls at headquarters, playing with babies, being so cheerful and helpful.

And me? I'd washed bowls and read a few stories too, but only because Vicky made me. I probably *seemed* heroic to the people at headquarters—just like I'd seemed heroic last year when I accidentally rescued Vicky from our snotty teammates. But none of the good deeds were my idea. Not one.

I'm not a bad person, I told myself. But what had I ever done *on purpose* to make anything better for anyone else? Nothing came to mind.

On the other hand, what *could* I have done? Ended the strike? No. Gotten Mrs. Whatsername's husband to a doctor? No.

Then a thought crept out of a corner of my mind: I could've called Linea—and I should have.

Jess was right to hang up on me the night of the Volkswagen incident. Linea needed her then—way more than I did. I bet Vicky called Linea. I bet that's how she knew Linea had moved away.

How embarrassing.

Of course Jess was disgusted by me. Not calling my own teammate when I knew her mom was in that Volkswagen was as bad as Linea calling Dad a greed-head. As bad as Corey and Joy sticking their tongues out at Vicky. Worse.

I suddenly weighed a million sinking tons of shame and guilt. Then worse as I realized that my droopy tiredness was exactly the problem. The people at headquarters who needed free soup didn't mope around acting gloomy. Even the lady who couldn't afford to take her husband to a doctor managed to laugh and joke.

A lot of those people had it way worse than me. Like the families of the drivers who'd been arrested. They must have been so scared. I wondered again whether Abe's dad was one of them. But maybe a kid who got in fistfights with boys from his team wouldn't *care* if his dad was in jail. Maybe he'd think it was cool!

No. Abe was probably freaked out. Anyone would be. If *my* father was behind bars, I'd be crazed—even if he *was* a total grump.

I couldn't call Abe, though. Girls aren't supposed to call boys. I flicked on the radio, but it was some stupid rockumentary about a band I'd never heard of.

I didn't have to hear Ricky Ronalds, though, to know what he'd say: "Try once more to risk the right thing." It was the line Jess and I always used to imitate. It had sounded so dorky before. But now it made sense.

Boy or girl, I told myself, people are supposed to call people if they know they're unhappy or in trouble or scared.

Like I should've called Linea. Like I should've asked Vicky about her mom. Like who knows how many things I could have done to make life better?

I leaped out of bed and grabbed the phone book. My hands shook as I looked up Abe's number. There it was. I dialed. It rang. My heart went wild.

A voice said, "Yo!"

"Abe?" I said.

"Speaking."

"This is Gwen, from headquarters," I said. "Well, not from *headquarters,* from home." That sounded so dumb! I was babbling.

"Hello, Gwen From Home," Abe answered, laughing.

Laughter's good, I thought. It wasn't mean laughter. "I, um, heard some drivers were in jail," I said. "I just wondered if . . ."

"You mean my old man?" Abe laughed again. "No way. He's not that kinda guy. Those jerks busting windshields—they deserved it. I say throw away the key."

I laughed too. "Oh good! I mean, I'm glad your father wasn't—What I mean is . . ."

"Hey, that's okay," Abe said. "And about the other thing? With the guys?"

"What thing?"

"Zack's lip and all."

"Yeah?" I said.

"Thought you might wanna know, we didn't start that fight."

"I'm glad," I said, blushing. I was sweating so much, the receiver practically slid out of my hand.

"So, don't hate me," Abe said.

"Well, I . . . Okay, so, bye," I stammered, then hung up.

Still shaky, still sweaty, I took a deep breath and marched into the kitchen, where Dad was at the table paying bills. "I'm calling a family meeting," I announced.

He didn't look up, just said, "Not now, I'm busy."

"Now!" I insisted, my voice louder than I'd intended.

We'd had family meetings before, to plan vacations and things like that, but I guess Dad could tell this was different. He put down his pen and followed me into the living room.

Mom started to protest when I turned off the TV, but Dad sat down next to her on the couch and said, "Gwen wants a family meeting." They both looked up at me.

Now I had their attention, but I wasn't sure what to do with it. Should I ask why they're acting so mean? Ask why they don't care about each other anymore—or about *me*? Just come out and ask them if they're getting a divorce? Just like that? I should've planned this better, I thought.

"Gwen, honey, what's wrong?" Mom said. She started to get up, but I waved her back down. Then Dad reached over and took her hand. I saw Mom's fingers wrap around his. They were holding hands! People who are getting divorced don't hold hands! Boom! Out came my tears in an explosion of relief, like fireworks.

Then Mom and Dad were off the couch, squishing me in a family hug. "You're *not* getting a divorce?" I asked.

"A divorce?" Mom gasped, leaning back to look at me.

Dad's voice echoed, "A *divorce*? Where'd you get *that* idea?"

"Oh, Gwen!" Mom said, tearing up herself. "We scared you! Honey, I'm so sorry. *We're* so sorry. We've been so tense, so worried, I guess we just didn't think!"

My sobbing turned into laughing and crying at the same time. Boom boom boom boom—the finale, with hiccups.

The next morning I called Vicky and said, "We need to play ball. You gotta help me round up all the striker kids. I'll get management. It's time for a game. A secret no-adults-can-know-about-it, no-adults-can-ruin-it game. Us against them."

"Cool!" Vicky said.

"Sunday morning," I added. I'd checked the schedule; the *Press Gazette* team wasn't on the road that day. "Ten o'clock."

"What made you think of this?" Vicky asked.

"You!" I answered.

Then I dialed Jess's number. Aunt Ann answered. "Gwen! It's so good to hear your voice."

"Same here," I said, feeling suddenly choky.

"How's everything?" she asked. "How's everyone?"

"Fine," I said. "When Mom gets home, we'll see how day three went."

"Day three?"

"Of her job," I said.

"Your mom got a *job*?"

A shiver went up my spine. Aunt Ann didn't know? Was that possible? Mom and Aunt Ann talked every day—didn't they? When had they stopped? I swallowed hard, then said, "Is Jess home?"

"Sure, just a second."

Then Jess said, "Hello," in a flat, dead voice.

"I challenge you to a duel," I told her.

"Huh?"

"A game. Sunday."

"Well . . ."

"Coed. Round up all the management kids you can and meet us at the field at ten in the morning—if you dare!"

"But—"

"No buts," I said. "You gonna do it or not? Yes or no?"

"*Yes!*" Jess said.

"And tell *no adults*. This must be in strictest secrecy. Got it?"

"Yes," Jess repeated.

"Fine," I answered, and hung up, my heart beating like wild.

Dad dropped me at headquarters after lunch. I'd never been so glad to see bikes in a bike rack in my life. And there was Coach Marty's car, so I knew Vicky had already told everyone. Inside, the kids were talking in a group. They waved and called out to me.

"No hot-dog stuff. Just softball, right?" I said to the guys.

Abe saluted. "You got it."

"I'm in," said Jose.

And Zack said, "Me too!"

I took a count. "With Vicky and me, that's five."

"Six!" Vicky corrected. "I called Liza this morning. It's Illinois, by the way, her *I* state. And guess what. She's coming to town this weekend with her mom! Something about selling their house or whatever. Anyway, she can play Sunday. And she *loves* the idea!"

"Wow! That's terrific," I cheered. "Did you try Marsha?"

"I did," Vicky said, frowning. "I talked to her mom. But Marsha signed on for another session of camp. She won't be back for ages."

"My little brother Nick's not half bad," Zack said. "I bet he'd play."

"That makes seven," I announced.

Jose said he could ask his cousin Juan, because Juan's mom was a striker. If both Juan and Nick came, we were up to eight players—one short, but it would have to do.

"Just remember," Abe said, "winning is *everything!*" And we all laughed, because coaches always say that winning isn't as important as how you play the game. Ha!

We were so excited that we went outside and practiced in the rain. None of the boys made a single antigirl remark. Not a one.

When we came back in, soaked to the bone, some of the grown-ups gave us a hard time, saying we could've caught a chill or been hit by lightning. All I could think was that if it rained Sunday, I hoped the management team wouldn't wimp out. I knew *we* wouldn't.

Vicky said we needed uniforms. We agreed to bring T-shirts with us the next day and use the art supplies there to paint them. And whoever could would bring extra shirts for Liza and for Zack's little brother and Jose's cousin.

"But we need a name," Zack said.

"Strikers?" Jose suggested.

"How 'bout that red circle with the line through it?" Abe said. "You know, that symbol for no smoking, no parking, no whatevering?"

"My dog had one that said 'No Whining,'" Zack told us. "But he ate it."

"What would ours cross out?" Vicky asked. "A newspaper?"

"Yick," I said. "Let's leave the paper out of this!"

We were all quiet a minute, thinking.

"How about if we were just team X, since we're playing against our ex-teammates?" I said. "Just a big mysterious X on our shirts?"

Everyone liked that.

I knew we weren't doing anything important or earth-shattering or strike-ending, but I was proud of myself anyway. Abe asked whose idea the game was, and Vicky pointed to me.

"You're not as dumb as you look," Abe joked. And I slugged him, even though I was sort of flattered.

Chapter Twelve
TEAM X—THE BEST

I DIDN'T HAVE any plain T-shirts, so I snuck into my parents' room and stole one of Dad's. He'd never miss it; he had a million of them. I considered swiping an extra one for Liza, but I chickened out.

That night I could hardly sit still, let alone sleep. My head was spinning with thoughts of the game. What if a fight broke out, like the one between the striker and management boys during *their* game? And what if Joy and Corey did more than stick their tongues out this time? What if it turned into a hair-pulling, punch-throwing bloodbath?

Or what if Jess couldn't get a team together? Maybe her teammates had church or Sunday school or something. Or what if Jess didn't even try? She might have decided it would *really* get me if she didn't even tell anyone—just let my idea die! Wouldn't I feel like a total jerk if we trudged out there for a game and management didn't even show?

Jess wouldn't do that. At least, the *old* Jess wouldn't. There was no telling about the new Hate Plague–infected Jess.

And what if the grown-ups found out? If Trina told her mom, Mrs. Johnson would probably kill us all.

The what-ifs kept me tossing in bed for hours, but I figured I'd had enough sleep over the last few weeks to last me a lifetime.

The next day was a blast. First Vicky made a stencil of a big X and we all painted our shirts. Then we practiced. Jose's cousin Juan couldn't come to headquarters, but he'd promised to be at the field Sunday morning.

Zack brought his "little" brother Nick to play with us. Nick wasn't little at all; he was bigger than me and he had a good arm. And he liked Vicky, I could tell. He threw to her whenever he could and kept looking at her all the time. Nick and Vick, Vicky and Nicky, I thought. Sounds cute!

We practiced hitting and fielding till we were exhausted. Then we all trooped into the air-conditioned headquarters to chug sodas and talk about Sunday. We felt like a team. A real team.

"Too bad it's only for one game," I said, thinking about the rest of the summer. The rest of my life.

Everyone agreed.

"Well, maybe we can dig up some other games," Vicky said. "Create our own league of outcasts!"

"Yeah," Nick said. "I know enough losers to make team Z. And my brother here . . ." He nodded toward Zack. "All his friends are weirdos, so there's team Q!"

Vicky giggled. I leaned over and whispered, "You're drooling," and she blushed like a tomato.

A couple of adults wandered over to where we were sprawled on the floor, and they asked what we were up to. Abe thought fast and told them we were putting on a play. "For the little kids," he added.

"That's nice," the woman said. "What's it about?"

"A league of losers," Abe told them. "Winning against all odds. You know, like that."

The woman nodded. The man looked at our drying T-shirts.

"Costumes," I explained, and that seemed to satisfy him. When they walked away, we all exhaled in one big gush, then cracked up.

Abe grabbed his guitar and came up with our team song.

Who are we?
We're X—the best.
X—the best!
Who are the rest?
They're nothin'!

"It's a musical!" Nick said. "Our *play*, I mean." And we all cracked up again.

• • •

I was dying to find out what the management team was thinking about the game. Vicky and I longed to spy on them. Then we sort of got our wish.

On the way home from headquarters Coach Marty, Vicky, and I stopped at the Rib Shack, and as soon as we got in the door, we saw Corey. She was sitting at a booth with some older girls. Her sister's friends, I guessed. The older girls were hunched together, talking, and Corey looked left out. I bet her sister brought her along because she *had* to.

Coach Marty got in line to order, and Vicky dragged me straight for Corey. I hoped she wouldn't stick her tongue out at us. But at the mall when Vicky saw her, she'd been with Joy. This time *we* outnumbered *her.*

Corey pretended not to see us for as long as she could. But she couldn't very well ignore Vicky bending down right next to her and saying, "We're *really* looking forward to Sunday, aren't you?"

Corey's eyes darted around, panicked, but the girls with her didn't notice. She swallowed and nodded. There was barbecue sauce on her cheek.

My feelings were a mishmash as I watched Corey squirm. Power was satisfying, but I knew how I'd feel if someone towered over me the way we were towering over her. And before all this strike stuff, I'd liked Corey. She was an excellent short stop.

Then suddenly I realized—she'd nodded yes! *Yes,* she was looking forward to Sunday. She knew what we meant! So Jess *was* getting up a team. There'd really, really be a game. Hooray!

"See you then," I said, hoping it didn't sound like a threat.

When we joined Coach Marty in line, he waved hello to Corey, but she was studying her plate.

"I'm glad you gals are staying on friendly terms," he said. I couldn't tell whether he was being sarcastic or not. We sat at the other side of the restaurant.

Vicky could have been way, way meaner to Corey, I realized. She could have gotten revenge, but she didn't. Maybe Vicky was immune to the Hate Plague.

I was in a Saturday-morning haze, shoveling cereal into my face and thinking nothing at all, when Mom came into the kitchen and told me we were invited to Gram's tomorrow for brunch.

Tomorrow? *Sunday?* Oh, no! I was instantly awake, my chest in a knot. How could Gram do this to me? Just when everything was all set. My mind raced. If I said I had plans, my parents would want to know *what* plans, or they'd tell me to cancel them.

I could fake sick, I thought, but then Mom would stay home with me—so that wouldn't work. Unless I convinced her that I was well enough to stay home alone, just too sick to go to Gram's. How would I do *that*?

"Are Jess and everyone invited too?" I asked.

Mom shrugged, reminding me that she and Aunt Ann didn't talk anymore. But I didn't have time to worry about that; I had to find a way to get myself and possibly Jess out of Gram's brunch. We couldn't *both* be sick; that would look fishy.

I went back to my room to worry. A plan—I need a plan, I thought. But nothing came to mind. Nothing. The more I told myself to think, the emptier my brain got.

I'd been crazy, I realized, to imagine that this game would really happen. If it hadn't been Gram's brunch, something else would've screwed it up. I couldn't be the *only* player whose family made plans for Sunday morning. There was no way two whole teams of kids could simultaneously sneak out of all their homes and get downtown to the field. Some of them lived really far away.

I sank onto my bed as if my pockets were weighted with boulders. I lay on my back and closed my eyes. But this time I didn't fall into deep, forgetful sleep. My eyelids were fluttery and wouldn't stay shut. I turned my face from the ceiling light and looked at the rectangular ghosts on the wall. I pictured the pile of ex-team pictures and trophies in my closet where I'd stashed them.

Then I was on my feet.

No! I wasn't going back to being a lily-livered ninny, or whatever it was Gram had called me!

I began to pace. Probably every single kid on both teams was up against something that might get in the way of sneaking out for the game. But no one had called yet to say they couldn't play. I wasn't going to be the wimp who wrecked everything.

I paced some more. I had to solve this.

We'd all sworn not to tell *anyone* about our plan, but I was stuck. And Gram, of all people, would understand how important the game was. Right?

I made sure the coast was clear and dialed her number. There was no time to figure out what I'd say because Gram answered on the first ring.

"Hi, Gram, it's Gwen," I said. "And I have a really big problem. But you have to promise to keep it a secret."

"I don't believe in secrets," Gram said.

"Well, but will you promise just this once?"

"No," she said. "But tell me anyway."

What choice did I have? None. So I told.

Gram made a strange noise. It took me a second to realize it was laughter. "That's my girl!" she said. "That's my Gwen!" And then we laughed together.

"So you'll cancel brunch?" I asked, relieved.

"It'll cost you," Gram said.

"Cost me what?" I asked, my relief evaporating.

"An invitation to the game."

"But, Gram," I whined. "It's not that sort of game, with spectators and stuff. It's a *secret!*"

"I told you, Gwen dear, I don't *believe* in secrets."

I was cornered. Trapped.

"Do we have a deal?" Gram asked. "One canceled brunch in exchange for one ringside seat?"

"This is a *ball game,* not a *fight!*" I said, hoping it was true. "Ringside seats are for fights."

"You're stalling. Do we have a deal or not?" I could hear the laughter in Gram's voice. She thought this was *funny!*

I took a deep breath, then said, "It's a deal."

Chapter Thirteen
PLAY BALL!

WHILE I WAS still staring at the phone, thinking I'd betrayed my team by telling Gram about the game, Mom appeared. "How's a trip to the beach sound?" she asked, all smiles.

"Beach?" I said, thinking, No! I've got to get to headquarters.

"You know," Mom teased. "Huge puddle with minnows? Sand? You, me, Dad, a picnic basket?"

"Oh, *that* beach," I said, attempting a laugh. "You mean today?"

"Yeah! Right now!" she answered happily. "Get dressed, grab your stuff, and we're off!"

"Sounds great," I said, and tried to mean it. We hadn't

done anything as a family in eons, and I knew they were trying to make it up to me.

At the lake Dad didn't pretend to be Grim, but that was okay. He and Mom sat on their blanket and read, giving me plenty of time to think about the game tomorrow.

I dug in the sand and wondered if Vicky and Abe and everyone missed me at headquarters. And I couldn't help wondering what Jess was doing. Was she excited about tomorrow? Had she been invited to Gram's brunch? Did she know *I* was the one who got it canceled?

When I saw kids swimming, walking, even passing by on boats, I felt a quick twist of panic, afraid they'd be management kids. I wondered if I'd still want to hide from them after tomorrow. Maybe the game'll change things, I thought. If not *cure* the Hate Plague, couldn't it maybe get the symptoms under control at least? Or was that a *movie* thought, I wondered. Just another "big idea."

When it was time for lunch, Mom unpacked all my favorite foods: burritos, apricots, chips, and lemon meringue pie. She and Dad must've snuck around buying all this, just for me. Mom never even allowed chips in the house, and I knew the quivering goo of lemon meringue gave Dad the willies. I gobbled up each treat while my parents beamed.

I spent Saturday night at Vicky's. We made what Vicky and Coach Marty called "tuna noodle casse-roodle," and we ate late, at the wooden picnic table in their tiny backyard. The sun was setting and everything had a golden, fairy-tale look.

After Coach Marty went inside, Vicky told me what I'd missed at headquarters. She said they'd practiced awhile, but it didn't seem the same without me. She probably made that up, but it felt good anyway.

"The boys have been acting almost human," I said. "And I bet Nick starts hanging around headquarters from now on."

Vicky shrugged like she didn't care one way or the other, but then she cracked an embarrassed smile. I decided not to tease her.

When it got dark, Coach Marty gave us each a box of sparklers—and it wasn't even the Fourth of July yet. I love sparklers. We made big Xs in the night, and sang as loud as we could: "Who are we? We're X—the best! X—the *best!* Who are the rest? They're nothin'!" I bet they heard us from one end of the trailer park to the other.

Vicky was a lot of fun, and if it hadn't been for the strike, I realized, I probably never would have gotten to know her like this. Well, the strike and Jess dumping me.

I wondered again what Jess was up to. Was she sleeping over at some teammate's house? Or maybe somebody was sleeping at Jess's, watching *Gone with the Wind* in Aunt Ann's bed. That would be okay, I decided. I didn't really want her to be *miserable*; I just didn't want her having more fun with someone else than she would've had with me!

Liza called about twenty times to say how excited she was about seeing us tomorrow and the game and all. I felt just the tiniest twinge of jealousy, thinking that Vicky was better friends with Liza than with me, but I shook that thought loose. *That* was the way I used to feel about Jess, I now realized, and I wasn't going to be like that anymore. The more friends the merrier, from now on.

I must've been making faces, or maybe I was muttering, because Vicky was suddenly looking at me funny. I quickly said the first thing that popped to mind: "I hope Liza appreciates her L."

Vicky said, "Huh?"

So I told her about how Jess and I had a thing for L names, expecting her to think it was dumb. But Vicky said, "I feel that way about names that start with P, especially ones that are tricky to sound out when you read them. Like Persephone and Penelope, and my all-time favorite, Philomene."

I laughed. "The first time I saw the name Phoebe in a book, I didn't know *what* to think!" I said.

Vicky and I were so keyed up, we couldn't sleep. Coach Marty kept telling us to hush, but we just couldn't. At around midnight I got up the nerve to ask Vicky about her mom.

"She passed away when I was three," Vicky said. "I only remember her a little."

"That's so sad," I said.

Vicky nodded. "I know. Want to see her picture?"

"Sure."

She pulled a silver frame out of her nightstand and flicked the light on. I blinked in the sudden glare. When I could focus, I looked into the eyes of an older version of Vicky. She was smiling and pretty.

"She looks like you!" I said. "She looks fun."

Vicky looked over my shoulder at the picture. Then she took it back, put it in the drawer, and turned the light off. In the dark she said, "Thanks," and changed the subject.

Then it was Sunday morning. I tried to eat breakfast, but my insides were all jittery. It felt like the morning of a road game, but even more so.

In the backseat on the way to headquarters, I whispered, "What if they don't show?"

"Then we win by default," Vicky whispered back.

"Yeah, but I don't want to win *that* way."

"Me neither," Vicky said. "I want to kick some management butt!"

Coach Marty shot us a suspicious look in his rearview mirror and said, "Hope y'all aren't up to anything foolish."

Vicky and I tried to look innocent, but we burst into nervous hysterics instead.

There were more people than usual in front of the *Press Gazette* building as we drove past. I hoped nothing particularly ugly was going on. I crossed my fingers and wished that whatever it was wouldn't mess up our game.

Then we were at headquarters. The first thing we saw was the row of bikes, which meant the boys had beaten us there. Jose introduced us to his cousin Juan, who seemed nice. But it turned out Nick had gotten feverish the night before and his mom wouldn't let him out of the house. I hoped that wasn't a bad omen. It was scary enough that we were short players.

"Nick told me to tell *you*," Zack said, pointing to Vicky, "that he's sorry he let you down."

Vicky blushed completely. Every inch of her. I'd never seen anyone blush that red in my life. It took all my self-control to keep from chanting: "Nick plus Vick—Nicky plus Vicky." (I did it in my head.)

Liza showed up a few minutes later and ran into Vicky's arms. They jumped around in circles, shrieking. Liza had cut her hair short. It looked cute.

We all compared nervousness. Vicky's palms were sweaty, but it was so hot, we decided that sweat didn't count. Jose said his jaw was clamped shut. My gut was all twittery. Liza said she had to remind herself to blink. But Abe yawned and stretched, saying, "Nervous? About what?"—so I punched him.

Then we ducked inside, snatched our X shirts off the table, and snuck out behind the building to pull them on over our clothes. Mine was gigantic, but so was Abe's. I wondered if he'd stolen his too, but I didn't ask.

Anyway, we looked pretty great—tough. Nothing prissy-sissy about a big black X! We planned our batting order, boy-girl, starting with Vicky, then Jose, Liza, Abe, me, Zack, and finally Juan.

We'd be up first. Visitors always are. It was creepy that we'd be visitors on our own home field. But it *wasn't* ours anymore; it was theirs.

There were now even more people at the newspaper building. We snuck the long way around to the ball field, to avoid them. And we didn't dare sing Abe's fight song, for fear of being detected.

We came up from behind the bleachers, and there was the

management team—right on time. My first feeling was relief that they were there. Then joy that there'd really be a game. And after that, well, I just wanted to *win* this game more than I'd ever wanted to win before in my whole life!

They were wearing regular clothes, not their uniforms. Probably because it would've been hard to sneak them out of the house on a non-game day. They weren't singing or chanting. There were one, two, three . . . nine of them—a full team.

"They're looking at us funny," Jose said. "Did you tell them you were bringing boys?"

He was right. Jess's team was all girls, and they *were* staring at the boys a little. I'd specifically said coed, hadn't I? Hadn't I told Jess that?

Jess. My eyes went to her and stuck. She was warming up, looking serious. I could tell she wanted to win this game just as much as I did. But too bad for her. I may have made a new resolution to try to make things better for the people around me, but that did *not* include letting anyone else win this game! That's for sure.

We were in two bunches, flexing and stretching, but mostly we were sizing one another up while trying not to let it show. It was quiet. I could hear birds. Then Management took the field with Jess on the pitcher's mound.

We got ready to bat. Every cell in my body screamed, Yes! At last. All I'd wanted was to play ball. That's all I'd *ever* wanted to do! And now we were really playing!

Vicky was up first. She slammed Jess's very first pitch and scored a glorious home run. Perfect start to the game! We screamed and cheered and went nuts. Abe gave me a quick minihug that made my knees feel weak for a second.

I peeked at Jess. She'd caught the hug and it made her eyes pop a little.

Jose hit a double. Then Liza struck out. I thought she was going to cry, but she didn't, and we all crowded around to comfort her.

Then, as Abe walked up to the plate, I saw Gram march up from the parking lot. Yick, I thought, Jess's going to kill me! Then right behind Gram came my parents, followed by Aunt Ann lugging baby Riley! Oh, no. I wouldn't have put it past my parents to bust the whole game.

I shot a look at Jess and she looked back at me. I knew we had identical expressions on our faces: shared panic and family embarrassment.

But the grown-ups didn't storm the field. They stopped at the bleachers and sat down. Phew!

I looked at Jess again and we both shook our heads over our loony family. Then we rolled our eyes and laughed at the same exact second. That's all it took. Suddenly we were cousins again, twins separated before birth. I felt a rush of relief like new blood through my veins—as if the evil Hate Plague germs had evaporated in one terrific swoosh!

It felt great—but I still wanted to win.

Abe hit a double and Jose was home! Two–zero. I was up. "Go, Slugger!" Vicky called.

Then I heard my whole team start to chant, "Go-Gwen! Go-Gwen!"

Well, I told myself, you wanted to play ball, so play ball! I looked out at Trina, down and ready on first. Corey on second, Joy on third. And right behind me squatted Nadine, their catcher, pounding her mitt.

I gripped the bat and watched Jess, wondering what she was going to pitch.

The first one went high, but her second throw was right on and I nailed it. *Pop!* I didn't stop to watch, but took off for first.

"Nice shirt," Trina said.

I decided to assume she wasn't being sarcastic, and panted, "Thanks." I wondered what her mom would do if she knew Trina was there.

Then Zack hit a grounder and I was off again. But as I neared Corey on second, I saw her turn her back on the game and start looking around! Huh? That's when I noticed the noise. I kept running. But when I got to the base, Joy ran away. "Hey! Come back here!" I yelled, but she didn't.

Suddenly the girls were abandoning their positions and running toward the *Press Gazette* building.

I wondered for one heart-stopping moment if the noise was an air-raid siren. Were bombs about to fall? Were people running for cover?

I froze, alone on base. Dad was flagging me over to the bleachers, but he didn't look frightened. Neither did Mom or Aunt Ann. I saw Jess trotting toward them, her hands over her ears. No one looked scared except baby Riley. His face was bright red and his mouth was a giant O! I couldn't hear his scream over the racket, but I could tell it was a doozy.

I ran past Vicky and Liza, who had their arms linked and

were screaming into each other's faces. When I reached Mom and Dad, they were all smiles. From there I could see a huge group of people at the newspaper building, hugging and jumping around. They were celebrating—not panicking! The noise was cheering and car horns! That's when I finally realized the strike had been settled.

The boys were throwing their caps in the air, then they practically knocked us over as they barreled past. Abe stopped and spun me around for a second, then tore off whooping after Zack and Jose and Juan.

"Isn't it *great*?" Vicky screamed in my ear. "It's our *movie*! All we need is the parade!"

"Yeah, but they ruined the game!" I called back. "What *is* it with these people that they can never let me play ball?"

Vicky and Liza stared at me, thinking I was serious, then they cracked up.

Just as Jess and I walked toward each other, the horns stopped cold. The silence made my ears tingle.

Jess picked up her phone and said, "Hello?"

I already had mine to my ear. "Hello. Who's this?"

"It's me."

"Hi, Me," I said. "You look sort of familiar."

"That's because I look like *you*." Jess smiled. "Want to make up?"

"Yeah," I said, "as long as you admit that we would've trounced you if we'd been able to finish the game."

Jess giggled. "No way! We would've squashed you like bugs."

"In your dreams!" I said.

"Your nightmares!" Jess squealed.

I saw Uncle Dave trot toward us all. I nudged Jess and we watched our dads throwing shy punches at each other. Then Jess said, "I bet you wanted to *kill* me when you saw Gram and everyone show up."

"Kill *you*?" I asked.

"I *had* to tell her," Jess insisted. "She would've ruined everything! She was going to have a brunch today."

I opened my mouth. Shut it. Then managed to sputter, "I told Gram about the game too!"

When that sunk in, Jess's eyes squinted nearly shut and we both turned our attention to Gram. She'd stepped between the dads and was holding up her hands. "Who's hungry?" she demanded.

Riley instantly switched from sobbing hysterically to happily chanting, "Pia Pee! Pia *Pee!*" He looked at Jess and me to take up the chant, but we were laughing too hard.

5/8/03